LUST

SEVEN DEADLY SINS, BOOK 5

LJ BAKER

© 2018 LJ Baker
All right reserved.

No part of this publication may be reproduced, distributed, or transmitted in any form or by any means, including photocopying, recording, or other electronic or mechanical methods, without the prior written permission of the publisher, except in the case of brief quotations embodied in critical reviews and certain other noncommercial uses permitted by copyright law.

ISBN: 9781792853128

http://www.lj-baker.com/

Cover by Pink Ink Designs

"Real life's nasty.
It's cruel.
It doesn't care about heroes
and happy endings
and the way things should be.
In real life, bad things happen.
People die. Fights are lost.
Evil often wins."

— Darren Shan

1

Luc noticed her as soon as he walked in the room. Her blond hair was pulled back into a ponytail as usual and she was sitting on the table, kicking her legs back and forth. She was laughing at something Harley said like it was the funniest thing she'd ever heard. He stopped in his tracks, watching her, and something swirled in his stomach.

Even before Amanda noticed him and waved him over, he had an overwhelming need to be close to her. It was like no time had passed, and he was right back in his month with her.

There was a part of him that wanted to turn around, walk in the other direction, and avoid getting closer. Their time was over. She wasn't the one, but he still wanted her. His polite side won out and he made his way over to the table.

"Amanda, great to see you. Are you making a delivery?" Luc remained standing, hoping it would be a short visit.

He wasn't sure how long he could be around her and not want to swipe her hair off her neck and kiss her soft skin. He knew what it felt like to touch her, to feel her heat envelop him, to be lost in pleasure with her.

And he missed it.

Damn did he miss it.

"Nah, just came to drop something off to Toby."

Luc glanced around, not finding Toby anywhere in sight.

She noticed, and added, "He went to make a call. Harley's been keeping me company. So how have you been? I heard your sister came to visit."

Luc nodded, shooting Harley a quick look, in hopes that she would save him somehow. "Yeah, she's hanging around for a while. How's school?"

"Well I'll let you two kids catch up," Harley winked behind Amanda's back and walked off.

Great friend she was.

"Sit, relax," Amanda said, patting the table next to her. "You look tense."

Because he was.

Luc sat on the chair furthest away from her and she scooted closer, increasing the discomfort factor by ten.

At least.

"School is going great. Although, studying with Toby and his new boyfriend around sucks. Have you met Zach?" She leaned back on one arm and stretched her back. The scent of her shampoo swirled in the air around them and Luc shifted in his seat.

"I have. He seems like a good guy."

"Yeah, he is. Toby deserves someone great like that. Though to be honest, I never thought he would settle down. I didn't think he had it in him."

She went on about Toby, his boyfriend, and her classes, chatting like they were old friends catching up. Luc tried to stay focused on the conversation, but he found it difficult to overlook the fact that not that long ago, he'd had his head between her thighs, making her scream his name.

"So what about you? Are you seeing anyone?"

Luc's attention jumped back and he shook off his wayward thoughts. "Me? Um, no, not really."

"That's a bit sketchy." She laughed. "Which is it, no, or not really?"

Since she lived with Toby, she could easily find out what he's been up to, so dancing around the truth seemed pointless. But Luc didn't want to talk about other women with her.

"You know, a date here or there. Nothing serious. How about you?"

"Nah. I've been focused on school. If I can keep up this pace, I'll be done in six months. Don't get me wrong, I like coming here every week, but this job can suck it." She picked up her glass, drank the rest down, and hopped off the table. "I better get going. Let Toby know I'll see him at home?"

"Of course." Luc stood and gave her a quick hug before she left. He wanted to tell her not to go, to have dinner with him, to spend the next week in his bed, but he just returned the hug and watched her leave. She wasn't his soul mate, so why did he feel such a connection to her?

"She's cute, right?" Harley appeared at his side, nearly making him jump.

"Was that ever in question." Luc grumbled and went toward the bar. He needed a drink, or maybe seven.

"Come on. I saw that look on your face. You were happy to see her."

"I was trying to avoid it actually. You really need to work on your social cues." Luc grabbed himself a glass and the bottle of bourbon from behind the bar. Before he could pour it, Harley was on the other side, taking over.

"Only because you don't want to feel things. You do realize that just because your month is over, doesn't mean you can't go back to one of the girls at some point, right?"

"I realize that."

If only she knew he'd gone back to see Ronnie before he met Talia. But the thought of going back, really being with one of the previous girls, hadn't really sunk in for him. Rationally, he knew that he had to finish all seven sins before he could pick one anyway, so it made sense that he might eventually spend more time with one of them. He just never thought of it that way. When their month was over, it felt finished each time.

"So then why avoid her?"

"Amanda has her own life now. She doesn't need me interfering and screwing with it."

"And if she's really your soul mate?" Harley poured herself a tequila, something she rarely did while working, and tipped it back in one gulp. "If you shut her out, you might never know."

Luc swirled the bourbon in his glass and watched it spin. "She's not."

"How do you know?"

"I know."

He had no clue.

Before he started all this, Luc assumed that he would know right away when he met his soul mate. He'd since learned that probably wasn't the case. He honestly had no idea what he was doing, or if he would know who his true love was if she slapped him in the face.

After being with more women than he could ever count, Luc never felt anything more for any of them, other than affection, or physical attraction. That was until he started this game. Each of the girls made him feel things he'd never experienced. He wasn't even sure what true love felt like. So how could he know when he found it?

It was part of the reason he wanted to pick lust as this month's sin. Lust was easy. There would surely be plenty of sex, and sex, was something Luc understood. The rules were simple. He was good at it. Love connection or not, the month wouldn't be spent having no idea what he was doing.

Harley was slicing limes, unaware of the turmoil inside him. There was a part of him that wanted to open up, to tell her what a mess this game was making him, but she would laugh. Harley was a great friend, but this wasn't the kind of thing he could talk to her about. Az was a bit better, but Luc wasn't sure he could have that conversation with his brother. Instead, he would keep quiet and hope for the best.

"You come up with this month's pick yet?" Luc caught a lime that got away from Harley and tossed it back to her.

"I've been wondering when you were going to ask about that."

The month had only been officially over for a few days, in his defense, and they'd been dealing with the whole Michael mess. He wasn't sure when that asshole would show up, so rushing into the next sin was irresponsible. And still, he wanted to do it.

"Now I've asked. Are you planning on answering me?" Luc drank down half his drink and waited for her to finish what she was doing. After the last fruit was cut, she wiped the knife on her towel, and stood in front of him.

"I think I might have some options."

"And by options, you mean you picked the girl, and found a decoy to show us with her?"

"I don't throw in decoys. You and Az need to get the fuck over that shit. I put a lot of work into finding the right girl for you each month, ya know? How about a little appreciation?" She raised one eyebrow and waited.

"I appreciate you, Harley. Even if you lie about decoys."

She slapped Luc with her bar towel, spilling his drink down the mahogany bar. "Now see what you've done?"

Luc laughed as she wiped up the mess.

"So, about this months pick?" Luc asked, hoping he wasn't about to be whipped with a bourbon-soaked towel. "When do I get to see her?"

She pressed her lips together and stared at him for a long moment, then gave in. "Fine, collect your brother and I'll meet you upstairs."

Luc finished the last drops left in his glass, texted Az, and headed for his apartment. He would pretend for a while that the whole world wasn't in jeopardy, that his own brother wasn't out to destroy him and everything he cared about. For just a short time, he would imagine that everything was normal, that he was playing a game, spending time with amazing women, and maybe finding his true love.

Sooner or later, it would all come crashing down. Likely sooner, rather than later, since he'd had a mage do some magic, which would hopefully lure Michael there. On paper, it sounded like a terrible idea to invite the monster in that's trying to end you. But it actually made sense.

Bringing Michael to him afforded them home court advantage. Oz, the mage, had things in place that would help them. Luc had access to the Hell Box that he would hopefully cage Michael into. Their people were there, weapons handy, ready for the battle. They may not know the exact moment it would happen, but they were as prepared as they could be.

In the meantime, Luc would continue living his life, because, well, fuck Michael. He had no right to stand in the way of Luc's happiness. He'd already taken enough from him when he had Luc cast from Heaven. He wouldn't get one more damned thing. This time, Michael would lose.

Az was already in his apartment with Harley when Luc got there. They were arguing over something Luc had no interest in, standing at the mirror. He couldn't decide if they acted more like brother and sister, or an old married couple. He figured he should keep that to himself.

"Okay, children, stop bickering." Luc walked between them and leaned against the back of the couch. He wrapped one arm around each of their shoulders and they shrugged him off at the same time.

Luc was ready for the month to begin. Harley and Az fighting wasn't going to get in the way of his excitement. The only thing that could bring him down right then, would be for Michael to show up. And knowing his asshole brother, that's just what would happen. But until it did, he would act as if this was any other month.

Az folded his arms over his chest and stared at Harley. He respected Luc enough to quit arguing, but he was childish enough to sulk passive-aggressively.

Harley rolled her eyes and waved her hand over the mirror. The usual fog appeared, as it waited for further instructions. You had to love a magic mirror that could show you just about anything, anytime, and any place.

Being the devil was a good gig sometimes.

"So," Harley said, rubbing her hands together like an evil genius. "Time for lust."

Luc's stomach twisted as the fog dissipated. He'd been looking forward to this sin from the start, but now that it was here, he couldn't help feeling just a bit nervous. The reason he'd put it off until now, was that he was afraid he'd get so wrapped up in the sex, that he would fall back into his old way of thinking, and not consider the girl as a possible soul mate.

He figured that by the time he was past the halfway point, he'd be over that, and into the groove of seeing past sex. Now that he'd spend the good part of the past few months getting hardly any, he was afraid his hormones would take over and cloud his judgment.

He was a man after all.

Basically.

"You ready for this, bro?" Az elbowed him in the ribs and waggled his eyebrows like an idiot.

He wanted to say of course, that it was the same as the other months, but it would be a lie. Everything about this month was different. The sin, his mindset, the chaos around him, even who he was now, compared to who he was just six short months ago, had changed. Luc was different and he felt it deep in his soul.

"Well, ready or not, here she comes," Harley said, as the mirror split into two halves, each showing a girl. "On the right," she said, doing her best Vanna White pose. "We have Annalee James. Annalee was raised in a small Midwestern town, by strict, religious parents. She is an only child, aspiring writer, and lucky for you, just moved here for an internship at City Life magazine. Her likes are puppies, drunken karaoke, and dancing in the rain."

Harley stepped aside and let Luc get a good look at her. She was pretty, but not overly so. She definitely looked the part of farm girl, with long, dirty blond hair, wide, brown eyes, and freckles dotting her cheeks and nose. She had a rebellious look to her that Luc liked, but she also had an innocence that he wasn't sure would mesh well with the devil.

"She's cute."

"She looks young," Az said. "And naive."

Luc didn't agree, but Az was entitled to his opinion.

"She's twenty-two, so compared to you two dinosaurs, she is young. Did you want me to look for senior citizens? I could scope out the local memory care unit next time. That way you could tell her your true identity and she wouldn't even remember it." Harley rolled her eyes.

"Okay, smart ass, who's behind door number two?" Az huffed, still holding a grudge from their earlier squabble.

"On the left, we have Destiny Smalls. Destiny grew up in Minnesota and recently moved out here to pursue an acting career on Broadway. Despite her career choice, she tends to be shy, probably because she was raised by overprotective parents, who home schooled her and her six siblings, giving her little opportunity for social interaction outside the home. Get a few tequila shots in her though, and she opens right up. Her likes include crossword puzzles, alpacas, and early morning jogging."

Harley stepped aside again and let Luc take a closer look at Destiny. She had a natural beauty that was hard to deny. It wasn't the glamorous, sophisticated beauty that Valerie had, but more a down-to-Earth, easygoing kind of look that was undeniable.

Her long, brown hair, fell in waves around her round face. Her full lips smiled, revealing perfect teeth, and she laughed with an ease that few could pull off. Luc could imagine her on top of him, her breasts bouncing as she rode him. He had no trouble envisioning the fun they would have together, but was that enough?

He took a step back and rested against the back of the couch, still watching both girls on the mirror. If he could choose, which he couldn't since he already knew Harley had made up her mind. But if he could, he wasn't sure he could make the decision. Both girls had something that tugged at him. It was the first time that he'd seen two choices and actually felt like either could be the right one.

"Clearly, it's Destiny," Az said, leaning in for a closer look at the girls. "She's more grown up."

Luc could see why Az would easily pick Destiny. She did look more adult than Annalee. He narrowed his eyes and focused in on the first girl. He wanted to reach out, touch her, see if there was a spark. It made him wonder about the other girls that were second choice, that he'd never gotten to meet. Could they have been the better choice?

"And what do you think?" Harley asked, with one hand resting on her hip. She didn't have the usual smug look on her face. She genuinely wanted to know his opinion.

Which of course, was when he wasn't sure he had one.

"To be honest, I'm not sure." Luc walked closer, waved his hand over the mirror, and switched to just Annalee.

She was in the park, perched on a huge boulder, scribbling something in a notebook. Her hair half-covered the side of her face, and she had sunglasses pulled over her eyes. He wanted her to take them off, to see what her eyes reflected back at him. There was a mystery about her, but he wasn't sure.

He wanted to flick back, see more of her life, but Harley wouldn't have allowed it. She never wanted him to have too much information. That was her job, to research the girls ahead of time, to know the things Luc didn't need to know upfront.

Once again he waved his hand, and brought up Destiny, who was sitting in a cafe, drinking a milkshake. She was alone, at the counter, and the guy flipping burgers behind the grill, was staring at her in a creepy sort of way. She seemed not to notice, fully absorbed in the vanilla goodness in front of her. She licked her lips and smiled.

Luc imagined those lips wrapped around his cock, as he held her hair back, out of her way. Most women had trouble taking much of him, but he bet that Destiny would work it like a champ.

Both girls were to represent the sin lust, so clearly the sex wouldn't be an issue. But there needed to be more. Destiny was an actress, shy, according to Harley, but bold when she needed to be. The sparkle in her eyes betrayed hints of adventure that had yet to be realized.

Being with Luc would provide opportunities that any girl he was with might never have otherwise. His status, and angel abilities, afforded him privilege that would be passed on to his mate. He wouldn't be allowed to tell her any of that, at least not upfront, but he could imagine a time where she would be able to benefit from it. Who would he most want to share that with?

Harley pushed Luc out of the way and switched the view back to both girls. "Well?"

"Yeah, it's not like I'm making a life decision here or anything." Luc folded his arms across his chest and huffed.

"Technically, you're not," Harley said. "I'm the one making the decision. You're just giving your opinion."

"What does it even matter? You've already chosen, so just tell me which one it is?"

"After you tell me which one you'd choose."

Luc glanced back over to the mirror at both girls. He didn't want to be invested in this sin and he wasn't sure why. He wanted to tell her it didn't matter, that if the girls both represented lust, he would be fine with either, but he knew that it did matter. One of those girls could be his soul mate.

"Fine, I'd choose Destiny." It wasn't until he'd said it, that he knew it was true. Az was right, she did look more mature. Maybe that's what he needed. Maybe she would have her life in order and he could keep the focus on getting to know each other. He had enough on his plate without all the rest that went along with these girls so far.

"See?" Az said. "She's clearly the one."

"I thought so too," Harley said. "She's a bit more set in her life, even though she only moved here last year, she knows exactly what she wants, and she has the drive to get it. She's not perfect, but she's on her right path. I think she could keep up with you, eventually anyway, and fit into your life."

Luc flicked his hand at the mirror and looked closer at Destiny. She was softer and rounder than the other girls, with wider hips. He could imagine someone like her as the mother of his children, if he ever had any. She wasn't a bad choice, but he didn't feel much about it either way.

"But I didn't choose her," Harley said. She pushed Luc aside and waved her hand, bringing the mirror back to Annalee.

Luc and Az stared at her, waiting for her to say she was joking. She didn't.

"You seriously picked that girl?" Az asked, squinting his eyes to look at her. "Are you sure?"

"Annalee is a little more impulsive and distracted in her life, but she has a good heart. She's a little mischievous, which I thought the devil could do to have around. She's not a complete mess, like you requested," she said, looking at Luc. "But she's not perfect either."

"I'm not looking for perfect." Luc stepped forward again and looked over Annalee. She was cute, in a bad influence, sidekick sort of way. There had to be something more to her though. Harley picked her for a reason, one that she wouldn't tell him even if he asked her straight out. He would have to figure it out on his own and decide if she was right.

"Okay then, this is your girl." Harley flashed him her *I'm-not-telling-you-what-I-know* smile. He was getting used to it by now. It was all part of the game. Luc just had to strap in and enjoy the ride, and this month, he had a feeling he just might.

He took one last look at Annalee before Harley waved her hand over the mirror, turning Annalee into fog. "How do I get to know her?"

"What do you mean?" Harley walked around the front of the sofa and flopped down onto it. "You need help getting to know women now?"

"No." Luc blinked a few times, taking the chair across from her. "I mean, she's not looking for a job, distributing alcohol, friends with Toby, wait, she's not friend's with Toby, is she?"

"Not that I'm aware of."

"Okay, so how am I supposed to *meet* her?"

"She's a journalist, well an intern journalist."

"So?"

"Do you ever check your calendar in advance?" Harley rolled her eyes.

"I'm not following."

"She's in your schedule, Lucifer," Harley said. "She's doing a piece for City Life magazine, you know, where she now works. She's going to follow you around for a week and see what it's like to run a club."

"You set that up?"

"Days ago. *You're welcome.*"

"So," Az laughed. "If he looked in his calendar, he would have already known which girl you picked. Sly."

Harley inspected her fingernails, pretending not to be proud of her sneaky set up.

"I guess that makes things a lot easier," Luc said. He *had* asked her for easier this time. He just never expected to get it. Easy was good though. He could do easy. Now he just needed to not only keep her safe, but keep his super powerful brother from stealing the Hell Tablet. Oh, and maybe keep Michael from killing him.

No big deal.

2

"Anna, you need to get out of there," Georgia yelled, while banging on the bathroom door. "I have an audition in like twenty-five minutes. If you make me run out of here without peeing, next time I'll just go in your shoes."

"Use the gray ones. They're worn so thin they give me blisters," Anna said, sticking her head out of the door, then slammed it shut again.

Three girls with one bathroom, in a tiny city apartment, was hell. Good thing Anna didn't care much for the primping and pampering the other two girls did. Shower, brush her teeth, a quick comb through of her hair, and she was good to go. If she was feeling adventurous, she'd glide on some lip balm.

Georgia and Destiny were a different story.

Thirty seconds later, she slipped out the bathroom, just as Georgia rushed in and dropped her pants to pee, without bothering to close the door. Moments like that made her grateful she had female roommates, rather than males.

She made her way out to the kitchen, which meant

walking the twenty steps across the apartment, and poured a cup of coffee. Destiny was at the table, nibbling on toast, reading her lines for the play she was in.

"How's it going?"

"Eh." Destiny looked up and shrugged. "It's not like I'm the lead. I'll have it down in a day or so. You're going to meet that club owner today?"

"Yeah, in about an hour."

"That's exciting. Which club is it again?" Destiny took another nibble off her toast and put it down.

"The Devil's Playpen."

"That the place on fifty-second, with the tacky neon sign?"

"I think so." She pulled a crumpled paper from her pocket and looked at the address. "Yeah, that's the place. I've never been there, so it should be interesting."

"I was there once. It's nice, crowded on weekends, or when there's entertainment. That's what I hear anyway. I went on a Tuesday. It was still busy." Destiny put her script down and stretched.

"Not really my kind of scene, but I do the stories I'm given."

"Life of an intern."

"I should be grateful that Sanders gave me this gig. Honestly, I caught him looking at my boobs, so he probably thinks it will get him on my good side."

"Pig." Destiny snorted. "Doesn't he know this is a bad time in history to sexually harass an intern?"

"I can't believe there was ever a good time in history for that." Anna gulped down her coffee and checked the cabinets for something quick to eat. Her choices were pumpkin spice pop tarts, or cereal. "We really need to do some food shopping."

"It's your turn." Destiny raised one eyebrow and picked her script back up. "Make sure you get coffee. I had to dump out the can to get enough grounds to make that pot."

"I thought it tasted a bit weak."

"Yeah well, do the shopping."

"Yeah, yeah." Annalee grabbed a pop tart, and her bag off the chair, and headed for the door.

She needed to catch the bus before it was too late. The last thing she wanted to do this morning was waste money on a cab. City living wasn't cheap and her savings were almost gone. Being an intern didn't pay well, and until she got a few good stories under her belt, she had no chance of moving up to a full-time position.

The only other option was to beg her parents for help. When she decided to move halfway across the country to a big city, she knew they wouldn't support her. She didn't know they would cut her off completely. *'If you're old enough to move out there, then you're old enough to support yourself on your own,'* they'd said. It was more her father, but her mother went alone with everything he said, like a dutiful wife.

It was always like that with her parents though. Everything had to be their way, by their rules, following their values. Anna had her own dreams, with her own values, and would do it her own way. Even if that meant starving and living on the street.

Hopefully, it wouldn't come to that.

So, she'd agreed to take this story, to follow a club owner around for a week, and do a *'day in the life of'* story. Or a week, in this case. She'd rather cover firemen pulling kittens out of trees, or the spaghetti dinner at the local VFW to raise money for the homes that got flooded in the last storm.

Or just about any other fluff story that didn't include her trailing some guy for a week.

If she had her way, she would cover real stories, the kind with meat, that made people think. But she was an intern and she took what she could. She just had to find a way to keep getting stories without having to fight off her wandering eyed boss.

Now she just had to make it through a week with a guy who named his club *The Devil's Playpen*.

Luc got a text from Annalee confirming their meeting just after he'd woke up. He wanted to reschedule, give himself another day to prepare, but it was just stalling, and he knew it. He'd had a dream about Amanda after seeing her the day before. In the dream, he'd asked her out for dinner, and she'd accepted. They never actually made it that far though. They ended up in his bed, where they stayed until he woke up.

There was something special about Amanda. She was tiny and fierce. Although she took a bit to warm up to him, Luc felt a spark with her. Maybe if they'd had more time together, it would have turned into something else. She hadn't been ready then, but maybe at some point, she would be.

Part of him wanted to postpone with Annalee just so he could go see Amanda. It would be wrong to see her after he officially met the new girl. This was her month and she deserved all of his focus. But it wouldn't hurt to sneak in a quick lunch with Amanda first. At least not unless Harley found out.

"Lucifer," Harley said, sticking her head into his office,

where he was pretending to work. "Your girl is here early. Do you want me to send her back, or should I set her at a table and have her wait?"

"Neither. I'll come out and greet her." Luc took a deep breath and got up. The chance to postpone was past. The possibility of seeing Amanda again, would have to wait. His month with Lust had officially begun.

The bar wasn't technically open, but Harley always let the locals in for their morning fix before she turned on the window lights, so there were a few people already there drinking. But even from behind, he knew who she was immediately.

It wasn't just the golden highlights that made her dirty blond hair almost sparkle even in the dark bar, or the same hunched over position she sat in scribbling into a notebook, like the way he'd seen her in the mirror, that gave her away. There was a pull, an electricity in the air, that drew him toward her, an instant spark, that caught Luc off guard.

This was different from all the other girls and it made him pause halfway through the room. Was this the universe's way of telling him she was the one? Would they have some love at first sight reaction, so he would know straight away, that she was his soul mate? He was almost afraid to find out.

Even though he'd thought this through, had wanted it for a long time, he wasn't sure he was prepared for it to actually happen. As if she could feel Luc behind her, she turned and looked right at him. There was no instant recognition, no lost in love eyes, no smile that told him she knew there was something between them. Just a quick glance, then she moved past him to scan the room.

Maybe he'd just imagined the whole thing. He wanted to find the right one for so long, he'd convinced himself he felt something, when nothing was there. With a deep breath in, he made his way over to her.

"You must be Annalee James." He extended a hand and she shook it, standing up, and flashing him a professional smile.

As soon as they touched, Luc felt it again, the electricity, the spark, the thickness in the air, that made him break the contact sooner than he normally would have. It was a bit unnerving, especially since she seemed unaware that anything was different.

Although he'd never admit this to Harley, or Az, Luc had worried that he *would* actually find his soul mate, but she wouldn't return his feelings. Wouldn't that just be one big karmic kick to the nutsack?

"I am, Yes, Mr. Morningstar. Good to meet you."

"Please, call me Luc."

She blushed, and the pink in her cheeks brought out her freckles, making her even more adorable.

"Of course." She sat back down and motioned for him to join her. "I'm sorry about being early. The bus that runs this way from my house has a lot of stops, so it's either early, or very late. I could have waited, if you have other things you need to attend to."

"No, no. This is fine. I'm all yours for the week now."

The pink in her cheeks turned to scarlet and she swallowed so hard he could hear it. He wanted to laugh, but he held it back.

"For the article, I mean, of course," Luc said and fought to contain his growing smile.

"Right, of course. So I'm not sure how much my editor told you, so if you have any questions, feel free to ask them."

"To be honest," Luc said, just as Harley appeared with two drinks, then excused herself. "My associate set this whole thing up, so all I know is that you work for City Life Magazine, and you'll be following me around for a week, to see what it's like to run a club."

"That pretty much covers it." She pushed her hair behind her right ear and nibbled on the top of her pen. "I mean, it's not quite that simple. They picked you because you're kind of a big deal, I guess."

"Something like that." Luc chuckled.

Only the King of Hell.

"I guess you're new around here?" Luc asked her, picking up on the faint Midwestern accent, just the slightest bit.

"I've been here a few months. What about you?" She flipped over her notepad and poised her pen above, ready to write down whatever he said. It wasn't exactly how Luc wanted to get to know her, but he had to work with what he had.

"A bit longer. Why don't you put away the notebook and let's do this a little more casual?" Luc almost wanted to try Valerie's drinking game with her, just to loosen her up, get her out of professional work mode. Of course getting her drunk didn't exactly help him get to know her either.

Annalee slowly set her pen down and pushed her notebook aside. "Whatever you prefer, Mr. Morningstar."

"Luc, please. If you're going to be following me around for the next week, I need you to at least feel comfortable enough to use my name."

She pressed her lips together for a long moment, then nodded. "Of course. I'm sorry." Before he could tell her not to apologize, she grabbed the drink in front of her and drank the whole thing down.

She was nervous and at least a little attracted to him. Luc had no trouble picking up on the cues a woman gave off, even when she tried her best not to, and Annalee was trying her best.

Luc picked up his own drink and tipped it back with one gulp.

"Now that we have that out of the way, tell me something about you."

"Like what?" She ran one finger around the rim of her glass, then slowly rose her eyes up to meet his.

"I don't know, how about something no one else knows about you?" Luc motioned to Harley to bring them two more drinks.

"Well, that would be just about everything," she said with a nervous laugh. "Maybe you could narrow that down a bit?"

Harley appeared with two new drinks and a bowl of grapes. She placed everything down and left without a word.

"Hmm," he said, popping a grape into his mouth. "How about, a secret dream?"

"Sure, don't make it hard, or anything." She tucked her hair behind her ear and took a gulp off her drink. "Let's see... okay, well it's stupid, because it's not possible."

"So? I didn't say it had to be something that could happen, just something that's secret, and a dream."

"I'd like to fly."

"You've never been on a plane?"

"No, I have, I mean fly, as in like a bird or something, with wings, ya know?" Her face turned pink again and she shook her head. "I told you it was stupid."

"It's not stupid at all."

Luc wanted to grab her by the arm, drag her outside, and take her up into the sky right that minute. He might not be able to tell her, but it was completely plausible that she could fulfill that dream one day. If she was the one. Not with her own wings of course, but with his, while he held her tight against him. He imagined just that for a moment and it brought a smile to his face.

"Your turn."

"Hmm, okay, but you have to promise to keep it secret."

"I think that's a given." She took another gulp off her drink. "Especially now that you know mine."

"Well, my secret dream is that… someday, I'd like to go home, like to my family, to live."

Luc had never told anyone that before. He was good at convincing even himself that it didn't matter that he'd been cast out, that he was fine living on Earth, or in Hell, but the truth was, when he was really honest, he missed home. He missed his family and the way things used to be.

"Are you estranged?"

"Mostly, yes. I have one brother, and just recently, a sister, back in my life, but I have a very large family, and the rest have cut me out of their lives."

"My family isn't big, but I can understand that."

Luc raised one eyebrow and she continued.

"I've dreamed of living here since I was a little girl. I wanted to be a writer, live in the city, and have some big important life. Now I'd settle for a full time job at the magazine, but even that wasn't going to happen back home." She paused and took a sip of her drink. "My parents didn't want me to come here. I guess being their only child, they wanted me near them. When I left, they basically told me not to come back."

"Harsh."

"Yeah, but that's how they knew to deal with it. They figured either it would stop me from leaving, or it would be easier to pretend I don't exist, than to miss me so much. So, I left and haven't heard from them since."

"I'm sorry. I know what that's like, but I also know that family isn't just about blood. If you have good friends around you, you have what you need for the most part. Not that it doesn't hurt to lose the ones you come from, but great friends can fill that void." Luc glanced over at Harley who was arguing something with a drunk at the bar.

"Yeah, I know. You're so right about that. My two roommates are amazing. I don't know what I'd do without them. Most of the time, it's good, but then I think about my parents, and it hurts."

"I know." Luc frowned. "I totally get that."

"So, the bartender," Annalee said, turning to look in Harley's direction. "Is she your girlfriend?"

"Harley? No. She's my best friend, my new family."

"What about your girlfriend then? Or boyfriend? I don't want to assume."

"Are you trying to find out if I'm single?" Luc flashed her a half-smile and her cheeks pinked back up.

"No, I was just trying to," she picked up the notebook and waved it around. "Work, ya know, getting to know who you are."

It was a nice save, but Luc saw through it. The blush on her face gave it away.

"Right, of course. Your readers will be happy to know that I'm currently not married. I'm looking to get off the market though, so they shouldn't wait too long to make their move." He winked at her and she sunk back in the seat. He was pretty sure she wanted to melt into the floor.

"What about you," he asked. "Are you dating anyone right now?"

"Nope, totally single. Completely available. And why did

I say that? I'm sorry. I'm usually more professional. I shouldn't be sitting here day drinking and telling you personal stuff about myself."

Luc watched the pink in her cheeks deepen into crimson. It only made her cuter. When he'd first seen her in the mirror, she hadn't stood out that much. She was average looks and nothing significant about her jumped out at him. Sitting across from her, he couldn't believe he'd ever felt that way. She was adorable, intriguing, and funny in a *not even trying to* sort of way.

"Maybe we should get out of here?" Luc suggested. "I think we'd both be more comfortable somewhere else. As far as not telling me personal stuff, well you can't expect me to open my life up to you for the next week without letting me get to know you, too. It's only fair."

"I guess that makes sense," she said, finishing off the rest of her drink.

"So, where should we go?" Luc asked, only *somewhat* hoping she'd say his bedroom.

"How about ice skating?" Her eyes lit up.

"It's a date." Luc stood and waited for her to join him.

"A work date... or not date. I... it's just work, right?"

Luc held out his arm and she looped hers into it.

"Do you want it to be just work?" He spoke close to her ear and she shivered. It was the response he was hoping for. She might not feel the magnetic pull that he did when he touched her, but he needed to know she felt something. She looked at him for a moment, then slowly shook her head, letting him know that she did.

He would take it.

For now.

3

Anna hadn't been looking forward to doing this story. Following some guy around for an entire week, just because he was rich and owned a club, seemed like a waste of her time and talent.

That was until she saw him.

When he touched her hand, it was like a fireworks show going off inside her. She didn't want to let go, hell, she wanted to rip off his clothes, and do him right there on the table. He probably guessed as much since she couldn't stop blushing. What was even up with that? Men didn't normally make her blush. She wasn't even shy, so her body's reaction to him made no sense.

The blushing part made no sense anyway. The wanting to screw him in the middle of the club certainly did. One look at the guy and it was easy to understand. He was everything Annalee was attracted to and more. It seemed unnatural to look that good. He even smelled amazing. When he leaned in to whisper in her ear, she thought she was going to come right in her pants.

Now they were going ice skating.

She wanted to die when she blurted that out, but he didn't seem surprised. He just agreed like it was no big deal. So there she was, sitting in his car, headed toward the ice rink. It was something she'd wanted to do since she moved to the city, but never got around to. At least she was on the clock, so not only did she get to do something she had been wanting to do, but she was getting paid to do it.

Plus, there was the fact that she was there with a super hot guy.

"You're quiet," Luc said and glanced over at her. "Is there anything you want to ask me for your article while we're just sitting here?"

She'd had a list of questions that she needed answered, but being in a confined space, close enough to smell his shampoo, or cologne, or whatever that was, her mind went blank, at least about work things. There were other questions she had for him, like what was he packing under those suit pants, what kinds of things he liked in bed, and what it would take to turn the car around, go to his apartment, and get him to fuck her silly all day long.

"So, you told me you weren't married, but are you dating, even casually?"

"Is that for the article, or are you asking if I'm available?" Luc turned, looked at her for an unnervingly long moment, then smiled. She was pretty sure they were going to crash, but at that moment, she didn't care. She liked his eyes on her. They heated her in ways that forced her to clamp her legs together in order to ease the tension there.

Without breaking eye contact, she answered. "Both."

"Never married, not dating anyone seriously." He pulled into a parking spot and turned off the car. "What about you? Do you have a few ex-husbands lurking around the corner?"

"I've never been married, so far anyway."

"Does that mean you're looking for something serious?" Luc turned toward her with an intent expression.

"Serious? Uh, I don't know. Maybe. I guess I'm not looking to have my time wasted."

She hadn't actually thought about being in a serious relationship, but if she did, it was probably what she was looking for. She'd had her share of one-night stands, casual relationships, and dating assholes for a few months at a time. Not that she was necessarily opposed to a few nights of sex with a compatible guy. Just that she was honest with herself about calling it what it was.

Annalee was never one of those people who bought into the stereotype that only guys could enjoy sex outside committed relationships. If people wanted to call that being a slut, then that was on them. She saw sex as a healthy thing, that two consenting adults could easily enjoy, whether or not they were planning on a future together.

And the more she looked at Luc, the more she considered it.

"Are you looking for something serious?" she asked, unbuckling her seatbelt, and waited for an answer before making a move to get out of the car. In fact, she suddenly wasn't in a rush to go anymore. She could have stayed there for hours, just talking and getting to know him.

"I am." He got out of the car and came around to meet her just as she stepped out and closed the door. If she'd waited a few extra seconds, he would have opened the door for her. She was glad she hadn't. She didn't want to set a precedent for that.

They got in line to rent skates. It was long, so it gave them an opportunity to talk a bit more.

"So, serious as in, settle down, get married, have a few kids?" She narrowed her eyes and looked him over.

"You look skeptical." Luc chuckled. "Don't I look like the settling down type?"

"Honestly?" she asked and he nodded. "No. You look like an eternal bachelor, who enjoys running a club and sampling different women every night of the week."

"I guess that was true for a long time." Luc frowned.

"But not anymore?"

"No, not anymore. I've been thinking about it for a while now. I guess the single life has gotten a bit monotonous. I want something more, someone to share my life with, someone to wake up next to everyday."

"What kind of woman are you looking for?" Anna pulled her hat down to cover her ears, glad that she'd thought to bring one.

"Are you asking if you're my type?" Luc elbowed her in the arm and smiled, as they moved up a few places in line.

"No." She pressed her lips together and blinked a few times. "I'm just trying to get to know you. Besides, I might put this in the article. The single women in the area may want to know if they meet the criteria."

She also totally wanted to know if she was his type.

"Okay, well I'm looking for someone who accepts me the way I am, who can be comfortable in her own skin and can make me laugh. My job can be quite stressful and having someone who not only understands that, but can be a haven from the darkness, is essential."

"Anything else?" They stepped forward, only about six people from the front of the line. She suddenly wished it was longer.

"Someone who knows what they want in life. Someone who likes to have fun, whether that's a night on the town, or curled up in front of the TV watching a movie. And definitely someone who can fit in with the people I'm close to."

"I didn't hear anything about appearance. You must have a preference of some kind. Hair color, tall, short, skinny, a little meat, big boobs, small boobs, ya know, anything like that?" They moved forward again.

"Honestly, I don't have a preference in looks. Women are beautiful creatures, no matter what the details are. If a woman is comfortable in her own skin, if she is confident, if she knows she's beautiful, regardless of perceived flaws, then I'm usually attracted to her. It's more about who she is, than what she looks like."

Anna raised one eyebrow and stared at him for a long moment until he laughed.

"Yeah, I know. You're not buying it. Most people don't, but it's true. I don't buy into the normal ideas of human beauty. I find beauty in all women, in one way, or another."

She wasn't sure what to make him him. Was he trying to feed her lines? She wasn't the most beautiful girl in a room, but she thought of herself as pretty. Maybe he was trying to downplay looks because she was on the average scale. It seemed unlikely that someone as perfect as him wouldn't also want a woman who was spectacular hanging on his arm.

They reached the counter and got their skates. Neither said anything while they found an available bench and changed out of their shoes. They stood and Luc wobbled a bit, so she grabbed his arm.

"You've skated before, right?"

"Yes, but not in some time." He wobbled some more, then found his balance. She found it amusing that he wasn't perfect at it. He came off as the kind of person who did everything well. It made her wonder what other things she would discover about him over the next week.

Arm in arm, they circled the rink a few times without speaking. Once Luc got the hang of it, impressively without falling, it seemed safe to talk.

"How long have you owned the club?" She'd rather be doing this with a notepad, or recorder, but if this was how he wanted to handle things, she would play along.

"About five years. It started out as a bar at first, but it's grown over the years."

"Quite a bit. What would you credit your success to?" She let go of Luc and spun around in a circle, then did a figure eight around him.

"You're quite the skater for someone who was so excited to come here. I thought this was some life-long dream by the way your eyes lit up."

"I used to skate all the time back home. Haven't been since I moved. So, your success?" She skated around him again, showing off with a few tricks she'd learned back when she was eight and considered the trying out for the Olympics.

"I don't know." Luc shrugged. "Hard work, great people working with me, and probably a bit of luck?"

She whizzed by him and he lost his balance, falling to the ice on his ass. They both laughed, but she could tell he was embarrassed.

"Maybe you should stay near the handrail?" She extended a hand to help him to his feet.

"That was your fault." He accepted her assistance, and once again, found his balance. "I don't need the handrail. Maybe you should stop showing off."

She laughed, then took off, speeding around the rink, and came up behind him, grabbing him around the waist. "I can't help it if I'm better than you."

Luc grabbed her wrist and spun her around in front of him. She landed in his arms, pressed against his chest. They stopped dead on the ice, close enough for her to feel his warm breath on her face. For a moment, she thought he was going to kiss her. She would have welcomed it, but he didn't. Instead, he tapped her nose, turned, and skated off in the opposite direction.

Ah so that's how he wanted to play it.

Anna thought about chasing him, skating more circles around him, just to prove how much better she was. Then she considered ignoring him altogether, skating until her lungs hurt from the cold, or until he wanted to leave. Then she thought about what it might take to end up in his bed for the night, and skated in his direction, slipping her hand into his.

He accepted her, without even a trace of his male pride being hurt, and they skated around the rink a few times.

"You said part of your success was the great people you work with."

"I did."

"Tell me about them. Who do you count on? Why are they so important to you? What would be different without them?"

Luc looked down at her with a half-smile before answering. "My best friend, Harley, is the one I count on most of all. She's been here with me from the start. It was actually her idea to turn the bar into a club, so without her, I guess everything would be different."

"A girl best friend, hmm. Anything going on between you two?"

"Are you moonlighting for a gossip rag?" Luc laughed and successfully attempted a spin, briefly releasing her hand, then grabbed it again.

"Just curious, I guess."

"Curiosity killed the cat."

"Good thing I'm not a cat, then."

Luc opened his mouth to speak, closed it, then opened it again. "There's nothing going on between Harley and me. *You* would be more her type than me."

"Ah, gotcha."

"You ask a lot of personal questions for someone doing a story on my professional life."

"You said we should get to know each other." She winked and dropped his hand, heading off toward the concession stand. By the time he caught up, she'd bought them both a hot chocolate, and they headed over to an open table to sit and drink it.

Luc took the drink and thanked her. He didn't seem uncomfortable that she'd paid, like some guys she'd been on dates with.

Not that this was a date.

"So, when you're not following men around, asking personal questions," Luc said, taking a small sip off his hot chocolate. "What do you do to fill your time?"

"I write mostly."

"What kind of writing?"

"Fiction," she said, pulling the lid off her drink to let it cool down faster. "Romance."

It wasn't something she liked to admit to. For some reason, it embarrassed her. She was trying to be a serious professional writer, a journalist, but in her free time, she loved writing sappy love stories. She could count the people who knew that about her on one hand. She wasn't even sure why she'd told him that, but some part of her wanted him to know her secrets.

"Can I read some?"

"No." Her eyes widened and she felt her cheeks heat. Telling him was bad enough. She couldn't bear to let him read any. She never let anyone read her romance stories. Those were just for her and not very good. It was just a hobby, just something she played around with to entertain herself.

"Why not?" Luc reached across the table and ran his thumb over the back of her hand. It was both comforting and exciting at the same time. She was torn between wanting to pull her hand away and telling him not to stop.

"I don't show them to anyone." She didn't pull her hand away and he continued to rub his thumb over it. The longer he did it, the more she liked it.

"You don't think they're good?"

"I'm sure they're not."

"Hmm." He pulled his hand back and she immediately felt the cold void where he'd been touching her. "I'd be willing to bet that you're wrong."

"You don't know a thing about me. I could be an awful writer and you wouldn't know." She fought the urge to reach over and stick her hand under his.

"Well, first of all, I'm a pretty good judge of people and my gut tells me that you're not. And second, I've read the magazine that you work for. They don't hire bad writers. They certainly wouldn't assign someone who was sub-par to do an article that they intend on making the cover story."

Cover story?

Her boss hadn't mentioned anything like that. Could he be right?

"You look confused." Luc took a gulp off his hot chocolate and tilted his head, as if he was trying to read her.

"What makes you think this is making the cover?"

"Chad called me personally and told me it would, when he asked me to do it."

So he's on a first name basis with her boss. She wanted to know if he knew him personally, and why he agreed to do it in the first place, or what else he knew, but she just nodded.

"Oh."

"I'm guessing he left that part out. Maybe I shouldn't have said anything. I don't want to make you feel pressured."

"No, it's fine. He's not a big talker. He hands out assignments and we're pretty much on our own."

"Not a great mentor, I guess." Luc frowned. "You must be good at working independently."

She shrugged.

Not that she'd given it much thought until he said it, but she was. Normally, she preferred it. This story though, had her feeling a bit out of her league. It was the first time she'd done anything like it, so having a bit of guidance would have been nice.

"So, what do you do when you're not busy with running your club?"

Again, it was a personal question. The story was about Luc as a businessman, as a club owner, and how he became as successful as he was. It wasn't about who he's dating, what kind of women he's interested in, and what he does for fun. But those were the questions she wanted answers to.

"There's not a lot of free time, to be honest, but I enjoy good meals, spending time with interesting people, and maybe getting into a little mischief." He shot her a sexy half-smile that made her want to find out exactly what type of mischief he liked to get into.

She was about to ask, when he looked at his watch.

"We better get back. I have some work I need to get to."

She wanted to tell him to screw work, come back to her apartment and show her the mischief he might be interested in, but she kept her mouth shut. They'd just met and she didn't normally take home strange men, but damn did she want to take home this one. Everything about him drew her in, made her want more, brought out an ache deep inside her that screamed to have him touch her. But she nodded and followed him back to the counter to return her skates instead.

They made small talk in the car. She asked him a few actual work related questions and they said their goodbyes at the door. She would be back tomorrow to shadow him for the whole day, but she didn't want to leave.

Tomorrow was so far away.

∼

"How did your date with Ms. Lust go?" Uriel sauntered over to Luc as soon as he walked through the door. She was dressed in a blood red, floor length gown, which was far overdressed for the club, especially in the afternoon. That was Uriel though.

"Her name is Annalee." Luc brushed past her and headed for his office, but she followed.

"Pretty name."

"For a pretty girl."

"Eh, she's okay." Uriel shrugged. "I liked the last one better."

"Well, then it's a good thing she's single. Why don't you give her a call?" Luc wasn't sure how he'd feel if his sister hooked up with Talia, but he had no right to stand in the way. He and Talia were just friends and if his eccentric sister could make her happy, then he would be all for it. Even if it was just a little weird.

Uriel scrunched up her nose. "I don't chase after women."

"Okay then," Luc said, taking the seat behind his desk. "This conversation is over. Any new developments while I was out?"

"I saw Gabriel."

"And?" Luc reached behind him and grabbed the bourbon bottle. He held it up in offering and Uriel nodded, then he poured two glasses.

"I was trying to convince him to come sooner."

"As I recall, he had something he needed to attend to?"

"He did. I helped with that, so he should be finished sooner than expected." Uriel swirled the drink in her glass, but made no move to drink it. Instead, she watched the liquid churn and slowly settle down.

"Would you care to elaborate on what was so important to him that it couldn't wait until after we saved the world from certain destruction?" Luc watched his sister toy with her glass before taking down half of his own in one gulp.

"Don't be a drama queen, Lucifer." Uriel rolled her eyes. "Michael isn't going to win." She took a small sip of the bourbon. "And no, I don't care to elaborate."

"Okay." Luc took another gulp of the drink and refilled the glass. "Then what are you willing to share?"

"Gabriel isn't thrilled with helping. To be honest, I'm not one hundred percent sure he is fully committed to our cause. However," she picked her glass up and sipped off her drink once again. "If Michael is really planning on using the Hell Tablet, Gabriel will help stop him. He has no desire to see the humans destroyed, nor to be on the side against what Father wishes."

Luc wasn't sure whether to be relieved, or worried. If Gabe wasn't committed, then he very well may switch sides. If Michael could convince him that he only wanted to keep the tablet safe, then Gabe might agree, and help him instead. There were too many variables, too many unknowns.

"So now what?" Luc drank down the contents of his glass, suddenly needing a bit of the dullness the alcohol afforded him. Even if it only lasted a short time.

"Now we wait. What else can we do?" Uriel crossed one leg over the other, revealing a long slit up the ridiculous gown she was wearing and Luc shook his head.

"Maybe you should dress appropriately for the battle we may find ourselves in at any moment."

Uriel snapped her fingers and was transformed into a warrior outfit, complete with weapons strapped to her hips. "Better?"

Luc stared at her with a blank expression.

"I realize you prefer to play by human rules, Lucifer, but I hold no such values, and it would serve you good to remember, neither does Michael. I'm an angel, not a pretend human. And don't you worry about me being ready. I haven't been hanging around on Earth playing club owner the last few years. I've been using my skills. You might want to brush up so *you're* ready."

She wasn't wrong. Not that Luc thought he wasn't prepared, but he hadn't actually been in a battle in quite some time. It wouldn't be a bad idea to get back into the swing of it, just to be on his toes. Michael was sure to be ready when he finally showed up. Maybe it was better that he hadn't immediately came when the mage set his lures.

Uriel stood, finished off her drink, and turned to go. "You

know, Lucifer," she said near the door. "If you'd like to spar, I'm always up for it."

"Maybe."

It might not be a bad idea to take her up on the offer. He just wasn't sure he wanted to find out he was out of practice with Uriel. She would probably have him on his ass in seconds flat and she would never let him live it down.

But better to end up on his ass sparring with Uriel, than with Michael during their showdown.

4

Sitting cross-legged on the chair in the living room, Anna scribbled notes in her pad, ripped them out, crumpled them, and tossed them on the floor. A growing pile, matched her growing frustration. Nothing she wrote sounded right. It was missing something and she couldn't figure out what it was.

"You know, there's this new fangled device called a computer. It lets you write things, then delete what you don't like," Georgia said, glancing at the mess with her lips pulled up at the corner. "It cuts down on the dead trees *and* trash on the floor."

Georgia had OCD. Any sort of mess made her crazy. Poor thing didn't know what she was getting herself into allowing Annalee to move in. Cleanliness wasn't exactly high on her priority list. In fact, she was comfortable in a mess.

"I'm old school. Just wait until I pull out the typewriter."

"What is this, the nineteen-fifties? Buy a damn iPad." Georgia pulled a hair tie off her wrist and pulled her long, blond hair into a ponytail.

"First of all, I can't afford an iPad, and second, it just feels better to hold a real pen, or type on real typewriter keys. It's vintage."

Georgia rolled her eyes and started picking up wads of crumpled paper. "It's stupid. You can use my laptop. Doesn't your boss make you write that shit electronically?"

"Yeah, of course, and I have a laptop for work. This isn't work, though, so I can do it my way."

Georgia spread open one of the paper wads and started to read. Anna jumped up and snatched it from her hands.

"Oh no you don't. That's not for public consumption."

"Why not? Are you writing some sort of evil manifesto, or something?"

"Yeah, exactly. I'm planning world domination."

Georgia tried to grab a few more off the floor, but Anna scooped them up before she could get to them.

"Seriously though, what are you working on, and why are you being so sketchy about it?"

"Just some silly stories that I write for myself. I don't like anyone to read them." Anna carried her pile of discarded ideas to her room and deposited them into her trash can. She could get rid of them later when her nosy roommate wasn't around to pluck them from the trash. Not that she would likely risk the germs, but just to be safe.

"So how did it go with that club thing? I thought you'd be gone longer." Georgia called out from the kitchen, where she started doing breakfast dishes. Not her own, of course.

"It was okay." Anna wandered into the kitchen and poured some juice. "The dude had some shit to do, so I guess we'll get started for real tomorrow."

"What's he like? I heard he was a total hottie."

"What do you know about it? You wouldn't be caught

dead in a club." Anna drank down the juice and handed the glass to Georgia, who took it without question.

"That's not true. Besides, I have other friends. Sean goes to that place sometimes."

"And Sean told you the owner was a hottie?" Anna laughed. "I find that hard to believe. That guy is the most homophobic moron I've ever met."

"Eh, he's okay. Maybe a little on the caveman side, but he has good qualities, too."

"What are they?" Anna hopped on the table and swung her legs back and forth, waiting for an answer. She was sure Georgia couldn't come up with a good one. She just liked Sean because he fucked her on the down-low. She thought no one knew about it, but everyone who knew them both, knew it. Not that she was going to call her out on it. That was her business.

"Anyway, I know other people who've been there too. Stacey went there a couple weeks ago."

"The chick from your office that you're always complaining about?"

"Yeah, her." Georgia turned off the water and wiped her hands on the towel. "I think you're just avoiding the question, Annalee."

"What question?"

"What is the hot club owner like?" Georgia pulled out a chair and sat, eyeing Anna's choice of seats with a judgmental stare.

"Well, he's not a great ice skater."

Georgia narrowed her eyes. "What does that mean? Is ice skating some weird sex euphemism?"

"What?" Anna hopped off the table and stood staring at her friend. "Did you forget some medication today?"

Georgia blinked her eyes a few times, not saying a word.

"Ice skating means exactly that. We went skating. He didn't want to be all formal and shit, so he asked what I wanted to do."

"And you just popped up with ice skating?"

"Yeah. It was something I've been wanting to do."

"Weirdo."

Anna shrugged and leaned her back against the counter. "It was fun."

"And what else did you learn besides the fact that he's not headed to the winter Olympics?"

"I don't know... he's single, looking for something serious, his best friend is a girl, and he does this half-smile thing that makes me want to climb in his lap and bite his neck."

"All great pieces of information for your article."

"I have a whole week for that."

"How long before you get his pants off?" Georgia picked crumbs off the table and put them on a napkin.

"Hopefully by the end of the week, or I'll have to find an excuse to see him after." Anna stuck her tongue out and walked away.

She wouldn't feel bad about liking sex. Georgia was no different, she just hid it behind shame and denial. Anna never understood that about girls. It wasn't like men were all having sex with each other. The good majority were hooking up with women, yet the men were the only ones who were allowed to be open about it.

There was a clear attraction to Luc, and she was pretty sure, he felt the same. If he did, they could enjoy each other, and explore where it might go. If not, at least she had some new fantasy fodder.

∽

AFTER A LONG DAY OF WORK, Luc climbed the stairs to his apartment hoping for a bit of peace before a new day began. All he needed was a few drinks, some good music, and to get out of the tie that was beginning to feel like a restrictive leash around his neck. He might even take a few moments to think about seeing Annalee tomorrow.

For a first meet, things had gone well enough. He'd have rather ended their time in his bed, but he reminded himself this game wasn't about random sex. At the very least, he had the next week to get to know her, to get a few glimpses if she might be the right one for him.

The physical attraction was there, on both parts. That much was clear. There were a few moments, when he looked at her the right way, that he was pretty sure she was imagining him naked. Luc laughed at the image in his mind of her face the first time she might actually manage that. The shock women had over his size never ceased to amuse him. Even for an angel, he had a lot to be proud of.

He passed Jason on the way up, and two more of the security team sat in chairs near his door. One was asleep, but he couldn't blame the guy. They'd been working around the clock the past few days. Oz had come through with gathering some mages to join the team and help to not only guard Luc's apartment, where the safe was, but to help keep the humans who populated the club downstairs safe.

Now it was just a matter of time before Michael made his move.

Luc punched in the code to open his door and immediately he knew something was wrong. There was a scent of burnt marshmallow in the air and the feel of dissipating magic. He stepped back out, kicked the chair of the sleeping guard, and barked out orders to get Jason and his sister immediately.

Seconds later, there was a swarm of angels, demons, and mages standing around Luc. Together, they entered the apartment behind Luc. Harley tried to push herself to the front, but Luc wasn't about to put his own safety ahead of hers. This was his fight most of all.

He didn't sense anyone else there, but it wouldn't the first time Michael used magic to hide what he was doing. They moved together, checking the small apartment. When they came to Luc's bedroom area, the folding glass doors that partitioned off the space were closed. Luc rarely closed them, and he certainly hadn't done so that day.

Uriel used her power to swing the doors open, revealing dark red letters dripping down the wall above his bed, that looked, and smelled, like they were written in blood.

It said, *I'm coming*.

It was just like Michael to stoop to such theatrics.

Jason and the rest of his team went to check the rest of the apartment, leaving Luc, Uriel, Harley, and Az standing there looking at the literal writing on the wall.

"What a dick," Harley said, walking closer and sniffing the dripping words.

"Blood?" Az asked as she stepped back.

"Yep," she said. "Wouldn't expect anything else, to be honest.

"How the hell did he get in here?" Uriel shook her head. "You have security everywhere. The mage put sigils in place that should have alerted us. And why not just attack while he was here? It's like he's toying with us."

"Unless he wasn't really here." Luc took a deep breath

and walked out to the living room. So much for his few moments of peace.

"That's his handwriting, Lucifer," Uriel said, following him out and settling herself into Luc's favorite chair. "He was definitely here."

"Not necessarily." Luc went to pour himself a drink. He wasn't in the mood to be polite and offer the others one. They could get it their own damn selves.

"What does that mean?" Uriel huffed. "If you know something, just spit it out."

"I don't know something," Luc said. "Not for sure, anyway." He made his way to the window and stared out at the street below. "But if he still has a mage working for him, and I'd bet that he does, then he could have managed to do that without actually being here."

"Makes sense that he wouldn't risk showing up here until he was ready." Az squeezed past Luc and poured a whiskey. "He might be a dick, but he's not stupid."

"If he's leaving blood messages in my bedroom, he's probably not too far off from being ready." Luc turned to look at the group of his family and close friends, the ones who had his back. "So we need to make sure we're ready for this. If any of you aren't sure you want to be in this, leave now. I won't hold it against you."

"I'm not going anywhere." Harley was the first to step forward. Her rage was like a charge in the air. It wouldn't have mattered if her death was certain, she wouldn't back down from a fight.

Especially not with Michael.

"You know I have your back, brother." Az slipped his arm around Luc's shoulder and patted his arm. "I'm always with you."

Luc already knew Az would be with him. He was too young the first time around, or maybe the last battle with Michael would have ended very differently. It wouldn't have mattered that their father forbid any of his siblings from getting involved. Az would have defended Luc with his dying breath.

Luc just hoped it wouldn't come to that.

Jason and the rest of the group gathered around. No one was backing down. There were head nods and muttered agreement from each one. Everyone had something to say, except Uriel. Something about that made Luc uneasy. With their track record, he would have liked confirmation, but he wasn't going to ask her for it. She would either offer it up, or not.

Jason instructed a couple of the demons to get to work cleaning up the blood mess on the wall, while the others returned to their posts. The last thing they needed was to leave other areas vulnerable. Before long, everyone had gone back to what they were doing before the ruckus.

Everyone except Uriel.

"Don't you have somewhere to be, sister?" Luc settled on the couch, since Uriel was still in his chair. He was ready for her to be gone, to have a few moments in his own mind, but she wasn't great at taking a hint.

"Not really." She propped her feet up on his coffee table, despite his scowl, and rested her head back comfortably.

"I'm kind of tired. It's been a long day."

"Don't let me stop you."

Luc growled low in his throat and drank down the drink in his hand. "Maybe you should let Gabriel know Michael is sending me messages."

"I will. I doubt it will make him show up any faster than

he plans on, but I'll let him know." Uriel popped her head up and looked at Luc. "Something else on your mind?"

"Everything is just perfect." Luc leaned back and rested his eyes.

"You can talk to me, Lucifer. I know I haven't be there for you for a long time, but I'm here now."

"Are you?" He opened his eyes and looked at her, hoping she would actually answer.

"Of course I am. Do you really need constant reassurance? What happened to you?"

"Oh, I don't know, my brother had me banished from my home, my siblings and father all kicked me out of their lives, and I've been basically alone for all this time. I can't imagine why I'd have some trust issues."

"You're completely right." Uriel leaned forward and rested her hands on her thighs, pulling her feet off the table." But that was a long time ago. Get over it already. I'm here. Either accept it, or tell me to leave, because I'm getting tired of apologizing."

Luc dropped his head back again. Even he was sick of his whining. The past was the past. He needed to find a way to come to terms with it and move on.

"I'm worried about Annalee's safety," he blurted out, not even sure why he would think about confiding in his sister.

"Because of Michael?"

Luc nodded.

"There was a time I would have thought Michael would never harm a human, that he wouldn't even consider letting an innocent get caught in the crossfire of any battle, but he's changed. I don't trust him anymore and I would be worried about the girl too, if I were you."

Luc would've preferred that she was concerned herself,

but he hadn't really expected it. That wasn't who Uriel was. At least she wasn't downplaying his concerns.

"Harley insists I continue with the game, and to be honest, after meeting Annalee, I don't want to give up, but how can I put her at risk with a clear conscience?"

"The devil, with a conscience. Wouldn't the humans be surprised?" Uriel chuckled and leaned back in the chair.

"Can we be serious for a moment?" That's what he got for telling her his feelings.

"I'm sorry. Look, I get it, this girl could be your soul mate. You have to keep her safe. Maybe you should limit her time here? This is where the tablet is, so it's safe to say that this is where Michael will initiate the fight for it. How do you get into that safe, anyway?"

"Why?"

"Well, what if you, ya know, die? Someone should have access, don't you think?"

"What makes you think I haven't already trusted someone with that information?"

Which he had. Az knew exactly what it took to get into the safe and had the means to do so. He wasn't about to spread that information around though. It would put his brother at risk and Luc wasn't willing to do that.

"Have you?"

"Why did you ask me what was on my mind, if you were going to ignore it, and pry into things you have no need to know?"

"I didn't ignore it. I said to keep her away from here. Get a hotel room or something. Or go back to her place. Isn't that what modern women do these days?"

Luc got up and went back to the window. He wasn't in the mood to deal with his sister. He shouldn't have said anything to her about Annalee. What did she know anyway?

The closest Uriel ever came to love, was with him when they were young. Then she chose their father's rules over her feelings for him, so it couldn't have meant that much to her.

"Sure, thanks. That's helpful." He poured another bourbon and drank the whole thing down.

"Oh, come on." She jumped up and joined him at the window. "Don't be like that. I really do care. When I heard through the grapevine that you were looking to settle down, I was happy for you. I want you to find the right woman."

"Does everyone know my private business?"

"Not everyone, but you kind of are the famous sibling, so people like to keep tabs on you. It's like the angels version for human reality TV." Uriel nudged Luc with her elbow. "Besides, I could win some serious credits if you pick the sin I bet on."

Luc turned to face his sister. "You're joking? Tell me you're joking. There are not really bets on which sin I'll end up with, is there?"

"I mean," Uriel shrugged. "I'm not the one who started it."

"Great." Luc shook his head and walked across the room, stopping in front of the mirror. He glanced at his reflection, not really interested in seeing himself. He'd been alive far too long to forget anything about that face. What he wanted to see was the face of his true love, whoever that might be.

"Is that what I think it is?" Uriel walked closer, touching her finger to the mirror glass. Her eyes widened and she looked at Luc.

"Not quite." Luc knew exactly what she meant. She wanted to know if it was the same as the one their father had. It wasn't, though it was close. It fell short in one very important way. "It doesn't look forward."

"That's too bad. It would help to see how things turn out, huh?" Uriel backed up, letting her hand drop to her side.

"Well, you could always ask dear old dad for that information. His mirror *does* do that. So if he doesn't already have all the answers, he could tell you with a few flicks of his wrist."

Of course, he wouldn't. Luc already knew that much, but it would be nice if he would. It certainly would save a lot of trouble, and probably lives, too.

"I've already asked him to tell me how all this will end. He refused."

"There's a real surprise." Luc leaned his back against the couch, still looking in the mirror. "Though I am surprised that you bothered to ask."

"He's not all bad, Lucifer. I know you've been away for a long time, but he's changed, mellowed out in his old age. I think if you gave him a chance, you might be able to patch things up."

It hadn't been long since Luc went to visit his father, to beg for his help in getting Harley returned safely. Not much seemed different about his father. He'd wanted to believe that could be the case when he got there, but by the time he left, he knew nothing had changed.

His instance that Luc give up his true love once her natural life ended, so that she could go to Heaven, rather than spend eternity with him, was cruel. It was exactly the kind of thing Luc expected from him. No, that wasn't true. It was worse. It was far more vindictive and mean than Luc thought he would be. His own father didn't want him to have happiness.

"You forget sister, I was just there. I saw no evidence of change in our father, except maybe for the worse."

Uriel frowned and patted Luc's arm. "I'm sorry things didn't go better for you there. I was hoping that you two could bury your differences and you could return home."

"Did you?" Luc laughed. "What makes you think I want to go home?"

He hadn't even thought about that possibility in longer than he could remember. Probably because it was never going to happen. That was until he met Annalee. For some reason, she made him think about things he thought he'd pushed down permanently.

"Oh, Lucifer. He misses you, ya know? And I know you must miss home, at least. Even if you don't miss him. It can't always be this way. You are both so stubborn."

"I'm not the stubborn one, sister. Father had the perfect opportunity here to extend an olive branch. He could have helped with Michael. Instead, he chooses to remain neutral, and risk everything he built, to that lunatic."

"But he has." Uriel took Luc's hands in hers and pulled him to face her. "He sent me."

It wasn't a surprise. Luc assumed their father had a hand in Uriel returning after she freed Harley from certain death at Michael's hands. But it was a small favor, at least for his father. Stopping Michael, or giving them a heads up when he would come, or even letting them know what Michael's motivation was, would have been real help.

Luc didn't want to fight his brother. He didn't want more to die. All he wanted was to keep the tablet, and the Earth, safe. Surely that wasn't too much to ask. Their father was the one who gave him the tablet to begin with. Why wouldn't he want to make sure it stayed where it was?

"And you think that was enough?"

"If anyone knows if it was, it would be him. Don't you have any faith in him at all?"

"No." Luc pulled his hands from Uriel's and turned away. "If you'd been treated the way I have, you wouldn't either."

"I'm sorry it's been this way for you," Uriel said. "I wish there was something I could do to make it better."

"You can. Help me defeat Michael and lock him in the Hell Box for the rest of eternity."

"That's a long time, Lucifer."

"Yes," Luc turned to look right at her. "It's exactly what he deserves."

5

An entire week, with a smoking hot guy, that she gets to follow around, *without* it being creepy. Who wouldn't like that job? Anna tossed a few things from her closet on her bed and tried to calm the nerves in her stomach. Everything was riding on this story. Unless of course, she wanted to cover the local animal shelter events, or sloppy Joe day down at the soup kitchen, for the rest of her career.

The article needed to impress her boss and he wasn't easily impressed. The guy was a dick. And not just any dick, the kind that thought women should get married and raise children, rather than have careers. He had to think they were living a few decades earlier, or maybe even a century ago.

The only way to get stories with real meat, was to outshine the men in the office. Her story had to be better than good, or even better than great. It had to be perfect. It had to shine. That was a little hard when all she could think about when she was around Luc was getting him naked.

But she had a week.

"Trying to impress the hottie from the club?" Destiny barged in and flopped down on Anna's bed. She was in a bra and boxers, with a towel wrapped on top of her head. Certainly no body issues there.

"I'm just trying to be professional."

And that was the truth. She didn't want to wear anything that would come off as flirty, or sexy. She already had only a shred of self control around the guy. She needed him to have no trouble keeping it in his pants.

"Well, then wear this one." She held up a skater skirt, that would barely cover her ass. "Oh, with this." Then she paired it with a cropped turtleneck sweater that would put her middle on display.

"I'm trying to look like a professional journalist, not sex worker." Anna snatched the clothes from Destiny and tossed them back on the bed. If only she could fit in Georgia's clothes, it would be no problem. Georgia managed to keep everything covered better than an Amish girl.

And she was still getting laid more than Anna at this point.

"Fine. Wear the striped sweater, with the corduroy pants." She pointed to the pieces sitting on a chair in the corner. "He will barely notice you're around in that outfit, because I'm guessing that's what you're going for, right?"

"I'm just trying to do my job." Anna picked up the clothes she suggested and held them up against her in front of the mirror.

"Well, if you're not interested in him, maybe you can introduce me? I don't need to do a job there, unless he needs a little servicing." Destiny waggled her eyebrows a few times and poked her tongue through her cheek until Anna tossed a sweater on her face.

"Get out."

"Fine." She huffed. "But I'll find a way to meet him, so you better stake that claim soon, or he's fair game."

Anna slammed the door behind her and slipped out of her clothes. She put on the striped sweater and corduroy pants, examined her reflection, and shrugged. It wasn't awful. It was plain and average, completely unnoticeable.

Exactly what she needed.

Now she just needed to keep her thoughts focused on the story and not on its subject.

∼

Luc noticed her walk in from across the bar. He had to do a double take at first. She looked like a teenager from the seventies. It was as if she was intentionally trying to blend into the background, when after just a couple hours with her, he knew she was born to stand out.

She was nothing like the other girls so far. If that meant that she was possibly the one, or not, Luc wasn't sure, but he was sure there was a difference. He felt it when he touched her, when he looked at her, or even when he heard her voice. The sound in his ears was like a melody that he couldn't get enough of. Sparks of electricity bounced in the air between them when she was close. It was unnatural, exciting, and completely unexpected.

Seeing her dressed in plain clothes, hiding her true personality, did nothing to change how he felt. The closer she got to him, the more charged the air around him became. He could easily imagine her without the clothes, so it made no difference. He might even have done a bit of that imagining early this morning before he dragged himself from his warm bed.

"Lovely to see you, Ms. James," Luc said, flashing her his best professional smile.

"Please, call me Anna." She shifted a messenger bag on her hip and glanced up at him through her lashes.

"But your full name is so beautiful."

"Well, Annalee is fine too." Her cheeks turned a light pink. "We can keep it formal-ish."

Luc took her hand and walked her over to a table in a quiet corner. Most days it was the place that Toby and Talia did their video game work, but today they weren't there, so the spot was free. It felt strange to sit there with Annalee, after he'd been there with Talia. She wasn't his soul mate, but he hadn't known that at first.

"Would you like a drink? Or maybe some appetizers?" Luc slipped into the seat across from her and waited for her to settle herself with her notebook and several pens.

"I ate, but a drink would be good."

"What would you like?" Luc held up two fingers to Harley and she started making her way over, in no particular rush.

"Well, it's only noon, so ginger ale?"

"And if it was after five?"

"I'd probably add some tequila in there."

"Let's pretend it's socially acceptable to day drink then. This is a club, after all. If you're going to shadow me, you'll quickly learn that we tend to drink like it's five pm, all day long."

Harley made it over, finally, and looked over Annalee like she was a shiny new toy. "What can I get for you?"

"Tequila and ginger ale, and bourbon." Luc kicked Harley from under the table to get her to stop staring.

"Sure thing." She stared a moment longer, then went to make the drinks.

"She's intense." Annalee let a small nervous laugh escape, then reigned it in. "So, what are we doing today?"

"What would you like to do?" Luc added a wink and half-smile, and got the expected reaction. She blushed. For some reason, he enjoyed making her flustered. She didn't seem like the kind of girl who normally had that reaction to a man, and he didn't usually go out of his way to elicit it from women, but again, she was different.

"I was thinking you could just go about your normal day and I could follow you around. You know, see what it's normally like for you around here."

The last thing Luc wanted was for her to see a normal day around this place lately. Who knew what that might include. Bloody messages above his bed? Demon attacks in his apartment? Break-ins, robberies, and murder? Those weren't the thing he wanted to expose her to. If he had his way, he would get her out of there, take her somewhere else like last time. But it wouldn't mesh with his cover story.

She was supposed to be shadowing him, writing an article on his life as a club owner. The story was important to her, so he had to at least make it work, but he needed to keep her safe at the same time. So that meant keeping her in areas where the mage put protections. It might not keep Michael out completely, but it was better than nothing.

"I suppose we could do that, but you have to have dinner with me after. So I can get to know you a little more. I don't really feel comfortable having a complete stranger around for a whole week seeing everything I do." Under normal circumstances, it would be completely true.

"You can just ask me to have dinner with you," she paused and met his eyes. "Without the excuses."

"Okay then." Luc's smile widened. "Have dinner with me."

Harley returned and set a drink down in front of each of them, smiled at Anna once again, and disappeared back to the bar.

"Is she hitting on me?" Anna looked after Harley, then at Luc.

"Probably not." Luc laughed. "But I wouldn't rule it out."

Anna took a sip off her drink and flipped open her notebook.

"Uh no," Luc said. "I thought we covered that yesterday."

"What?"

"The notes. Just relax and keep it casual." He nodded his head at her pad and took a long swallow of his bourbon. "Just two people, getting to know each other. I would be willing to bet that by the end of the week, you'll have no trouble writing your article if you stick that thing back in your bag and experience this with me."

"It's just that I—"

"How about this? If you don't feel like you have enough by the end of the week, you can stay a whole other week and take all the notes you want?"

He watched her ponder the options in her head. His temples tingled with the desire to look inside her mind, to see what she was thinking, but he held back as always.

"I only have two weeks to do my research, write the story, and hand it in."

"So, you can take notes for five days then, and the last two will be to write... if you don't have brilliant ideas by the end of the first week that is. Deal?"

He kind of hoped she didn't feel prepared at the end of the first week, so he would have an excuse to have her around longer. But more so, he hoped that by the end of the week, he wouldn't need excuses to keep her around.

"Okay, deal." She held out her hand to shake on it and he accepted. "And I get to pick dinner."

"For tonight, anyway." Luc gulped down the rest of his bourbon and winked again. She didn't blush this time. He was a bit disappointed. He was starting to enjoy the way her cheeks pinked. It made him think about how they would look in the throes of passion and he couldn't wait to see the comparison up close and personal.

"Oh, so you think you're going to get multiple dinners out of this deal?"

"I hope so."

She took a few sips off her drink and they sat in awkward silence for a solid minute. Luc actually enjoyed the reprieve. She wasn't one of those girls who felt the need to fill every second with chatter. Awkward or not, she sat with it, tolerated the quiet, and relaxed more and more as the seconds ticked by.

Several locals started to wander in and take their usual spots at the bar. Harley served them drinks without a word. She memorized every order and anticipated their needs before they even knew what they were. For a demon, she was a damn good bartender.

"So, do you sit around and drink all day? Or do you actually do some work around here?" Anna asked, finishing off half her drink. The alcohol gave her courage, but the attitude was all hers.

"Sure, I do work, smart ass. Finish up your watered down tequila and we can get to it."

"It's not watered down. It's ginger ale. Sorry I'm not a fan of that nasty shit you drink."

Luc held his hand over his heart. "You did not just call my perfectly aged bourbon, *nasty shit*?"

"I did. I'm guessing you had some sort of accident, or

illness, so you can't taste how bad it actually is. So really, it's probably not your fault." She gulped down the rest of her drink and pushed the glass at him. "Okay, done. Let's get to work."

Luc stared at her for a long moment.

She didn't like his favorite drink. She enjoyed ice skating, something he wasn't a fan of. He wondered what else they wouldn't agree on. So far, it wasn't looking good. But then when he looked at her, none of it mattered. The pull between them was strong enough that he could drink a tequila with ginger ale and be perfectly satisfied.

At least as far as alcohol went.

"Try not to get in the way." Luc got up and headed for the storeroom out back, without turning to see if she was following. He didn't need to. He could feel the pull of her behind him and he wondered if she felt it too.

This was going to be an interesting week.

~

IT TOOK everything she had in her to keep focused on work. The drinking didn't help. She was going to have to limit her alcohol intake around him, or she was going to need that second week, not because she couldn't take notes, but because she spent the whole first week day dreaming about having him bend her over one of these cases of whiskey to take her from behind.

He led her toward a delivery bay where a tough looking blond chick was arguing with some dude twice her size. He literally looked like he could break her in half, but she wasn't backing down. Anna couldn't help but admire that kind of spunk.

"Sorry about this. I have to see what's going on," Luc said, turning to speak to her.

"Don't apologize. You're supposed to be doing what you would normally be doing, so ignore me and have at it."

He smiled and nodded, then composed himself into he professional businessman, and headed down the the two arguing.

"Amanda, Xavier, what is going on?"

There was a look that passed between Luc and the woman when she noticed Anna standing behind Luc like some lost puppy dog. It was the kind of look exes gave each other when they saw them with someone new. There was definitely a vibe between them, but it was none of her business. She was there to observe, not get into his personal business.

"He unloaded my shit and now he's saying I was short a box. I'm never short. I counted it myself." She stood with one hand on her hip and the other balled into a fist at her side. She didn't look like the kind of girl you messed with, even if you were a six foot six dude, who weighed at least two-eighty.

"Everyone makes mistakes." Xavier wasn't backing down.

"That includes you," Luc said to the large man. "If Amanda says there was another box, then I'm sure there was. Go back and recount them."

The guy looked like he was about to argue, but Luc pressed his lips together and started right at him. The guy stood his ground for another few seconds, then let out a puff of air, and stormed off.

"Sorry about that. Xavier is new here. We've had some turnover since you started delivering here."

"That's fine," she said, looking past him and sizing Anna up. "She new too?"

"No. This is Annalee James." Luc held his arm out welcoming her over. "She's an up and coming journalist for City Life Magazine. She's doing a story on me."

"Amanda Mitchell." She held her hand out and Anna took it for a quick shake. "Good luck with the story. Just watch out for this one's charm." She motioned her thumb in Luc's direction and smiled.

"Maybe I should interview you, get some opinions from others who work with Luc," Anna said, more because she was curious about the woman, but it wouldn't be a bad idea either.

"Sounds great." Amanda handed her a business card just as the big guy returned.

"I miscounted. Sorry." He kept his head bowed, avoiding looking at Amanda, or Luc.

"See," Luc said. "All fixed." Xavier stalked away, mumbling something under his breath that caught Luc's attention. He didn't say anything, but Anna got the idea that it wouldn't be left that way.

"All good?" Luc asked Amanda and she nodded, handing over a clipboard for him to sign.

She paused a moment, like she wanted to say something more, but stopped herself. Luc had the same look about him, but she let it drop, and was out the door before he could stop her.

"You and her have a thing going on?" Anna asked as he watched Amanda get into her van and pull away.

"There was something, for like a minute, but we weren't right for each other. She's on a different path." He took her arm and led her out of the delivery bay.

"Do you regret it?"

He stopped and looked at her, no, more searched her,

like he was digging into her soul, trying to find some answer that she didn't have.

"No," he said, finally, putting both hands on her arms. "If Amanda and I tried to make things work, I would never have met you. That, I would have regretted."

The whole thing only lasted about thirty seconds, but it felt much longer. The impact remained, long after he let go and started off toward the way back again. She could still feel his hands gripping her arms, feel the warmth of his breath on her face, sense the connection between them that she'd thought she imagined. It was more than she expected and she wasn't sure what to make of it.

They'd only met yesterday and she'd spent most of the time since having dirty thoughts about him. But that, just now, that was something else, something she didn't know how to define, and she wasn't sure if she should be afraid of it, or welcome it.

"We get several deliveries a week, from each of a few vendors we use," Luc started talking, but she was only half absorbing the information. "Amanda is one of the smaller ones, local stuff mostly, but the patrons like what she brings us. Harley usually handles most of that stuff, but the other day-bartender called out today, so she needs to stay up there."

"I bet this place goes through a lot of alcohol," she said, trying to make it seem like she hadn't just been thrown off her axis, and tossed into the twilight zone.

"We do, yeah, but also a lot of bottled water and soda. The place gets busy at night and weekends are insane."

They passed several employees as they walked. A few stopped Luc to ask him questions, or to have him sign something. One said he needed to speak with him privately later. And another just wanted to flirt with him. He was cordial, but firm, every bit the serious businessman that he looked in his expensive suit.

"This is where the magic happens." He led her into a small office, that didn't look anywhere near lavish enough for someone of his status.

The room was just big enough to have a large desk, a few chairs, a small sofa, and a mini-bar. She should have guessed there would be alcohol there as well. The guy drank like an alcoholic so far in the short time she'd known him. She would probably leave that impression out of her article though.

"This place is huge. Couldn't you have found a bigger workspace?" She wandered around the small room and looked at the art hanging around them. The artist was talented. Each piece invited you in, caught your attention, and made the kind of impression that left you wanting to know more.

"I didn't need more. This works." Luc shrugged and sat on the corner of his desk.

Anna stopped to admire a framed sketch of Luc overlooking a cliff, in what appeared to be paradise. "You know the artist?"

"Valerie Kensington, yes. She's very talented.

"Another ex-girlfriend?"

"I wouldn't call her that." Luc frowned and crossed his arms over his chest.

"What would you call her?"

"Someone I was lucky enough to get to know for a short while."

"What will you say about me, after I'm gone, and someone asks about the girl who wrote the article about you?" Anna turned to look at him.

"I don't know yet." He pushed off the desk and came over

to her. He put one hand up to her face and pulled it toward his. "I'll have to get back to you on that."

Anna's heart jumped into overdrive and her breathing became shallow. Her body was screaming for more contact, but he hovered just inches away, showing no signs of taking it further. If she read him right, he could wait there all night. She had no such patience.

She slipped her hand behind his neck and pulled his mouth down on hers. He needed no further encouragement, taking control of the kiss, and making her legs go weak. If that was how he kissed, she wasn't sure she would survive more, but she damn sure wanted to find out.

Much sooner than she wanted, he pulled back, and broke the kiss. She was literally panting, silently begging for him to continue. He smiled, that sexy, half-smile, that told her he knew exactly what effect he had on her. Normally, she liked having the upper hand, making guys crawl on their knees to her, beg her for more. There was none of that here. She would gladly be the one on her knees.

He ran his thumb over her bottom lip, wetting it with their mixed saliva, then pulled her hard against him, crushing their bodies together. His arousal was pinned between them, proving to her that she wasn't the only one who wanted more. He'd done it on purpose, for just that reason. He wanted her to know the effect she had on him as well.

Anna glanced at the door and wondered if it locked. How long before someone would come looking for them? Would a quickie in his tiny office even be enough to satisfy her? Not that she had anything against quickies, but the intensity of her desire for him told her she needed more, more than a few minutes of intense fucking, more than whatever they could squeeze in before someone knocked on the door. She wanted hours, maybe even days, to explore his body, milk the electricity between them for all it was worth.

Luc turned, to follow her gaze. His smile widened, spanning his face from ear, to ear. He knew exactly what she was thinking and he liked the idea.

"Is this a part of your daily routine?" she asked him, her voice barely above a whisper, and her heart still slamming against her chest.

"No, but I wouldn't mind making it one."

They stood there, locked in that moment, both wanting more, neither taking the step to make it happen. She expected he would, after they kissed, but he didn't. He waited, as he had with the kiss. Was he expecting her to make the first move, to decide it was what she wanted? He had to know she had no doubts.

She glanced at the door again.

The heat in her middle spread. Her arms tingled and her fingers felt numb. She'd never wanted anyone so badly in her life, yet she stood there, looking at him, watching his eyes as they focused on her lips. She could tell him to fuck her and that would be it. It would be enough. But her voice refused to cooperate. She could grab his cock, feel him through his pants, and her intentions would be clear, but she didn't.

Minutes ticked by, and they stood there, locked in an embrace, staring into each other, hearts jacked up, breathing in pants. The mutual desire laid in the air like a thick blanket, weighing her down. She wasn't shy, and she had no problem letting a man know exactly what she wanted, but for some reason, with Luc, she couldn't seem to take the jump.

Just when she thought she would scream, or finally push him down on the couch to climb in his lap, there was a knock on the door, followed by a blond guy poking his head into the office.

"Hey Luc, do you got a—"

Luc didn't move. He didn't let her go, or stop looking at her lips. He did smile, which made her smile, and they knew their moment was over. She wiggled out of his arms and crossed her own over her chest.

"Sorry, I didn't realize you had company." The guy tried to leave, but Luc stopped him.

"It's fine. Come in." Luc walked behind the desk and pulled out a couple water bottles from a small fridge. He handed her one and drank down half of his own. "This is my brother, Azrael."

"Az." The guy stepped forward and extended a hand, which she shook, hoping her face wasn't as red as it felt.

"Az, this is Annalee James. She's writing the article I told you about."

"Ah," he said and nodded his head. "Nice to meet you." He held her hand a moment too long, then turned to Luc. "Find me later. There's something I'd like to go over with you."

"Anything pressing?"

"Nah, it can wait." Az turned to look at Anna once more. "Do what you gotta do." Then he left, clicking the door closed behind him.

"Is there anyone in your family that doesn't look like an airbrushed supermodel?" She sunk down onto the couch, with her arms wrapped around her middle. It was the only thing containing whatever it was inside her that wanted to leap out and impale her on Luc.

"No probably not. We're lucky, I guess."

There was a twinkle in his eye that told her there was something more that she wasn't getting, but she didn't care.

The room was suddenly too small, too close, too thick with arousal. It made her want to jump out of her skin.

The week had just begun and she had to spend the next six days with this guy. If she jumped him now, and things didn't work out, the week would be miserable. In turn, her story would suffer because of it. She wanted to keep things professional, at least until she had enough to write a great article, but she was pretty sure that was going to be impossible.

6

No day had ever passed more slowly, not even in Hell where time worked differently. All Luc wanted all day was to drag Anna upstairs and fuck her senseless, but he was afraid to bring her up there. If Michael could manage to find a way to write him a message on his wall, who knew what else he could do? Besides, the apartment wasn't protected the way the club was. Michael would be able to get in and Luc refused to put Anna at additional risk.

So he showed her around, taught her how he did paperwork, handled deliveries, even had Harley teach her how to make a few drinks. She was having fun. He could tell that she was, but that look was there, the need that hung between them before his idiot brother interrupted them, had only dampened a bit.

He could have had her naked and pinned to the wall right after she kissed him. She'd wanted it and he was beyond ready to have her. But he'd let too many thoughts into his head. What if she was the one? Did he want his first time with his soul mate to be a quickie in his office, that his brother would have walked in on?

Every moment should be special, memorable, something that they would both have, long after they didn't have each other. His father's punishment tainted it, and took something from him that even now, before he knew who the right one was, he could never have back.

Luc leaned against the wall watching her. She was laughing at something Uriel said, while Harley was teaching her to toss bottles in the air and catch them. She'd broken four so far, but was finally starting to get the hang of it. Az was sitting on a barstool, cheering her on.

The scene made Luc take pause. His family, and when he said family, he meant the three people surrounding Anna at that very moment, those people, who meant the most to him in the world, liked this woman, embraced her, welcomed her in. There was something so endearing about it. He would say touching, but he was the devil, and he had to have some dignity.

He could have stayed there all day, watching her laugh, have fun, enjoy the world without knowing about Hell Tablets, or Angel battles, or just how many evils there were in the world, but she saw him and waved him over. The way her face lit up made her unable to ignore. He took one last moment to enjoy the brightness she brought into the place and walked over.

"Trashing my bar, I see," Luc said glancing in a bucket of broken glass.

"Yeah, it's awesome. Watch." She flipped a bottle up, it spun, and she caught it. Then it slipped from her hand and smashed on the floor. "Okay, well I need some practice." She laughed, unconcerned with the failure, the broken glass, or anything else other than having fun.

"I'd say so, yes." Luc settled on a stool between his siblings and took a gulp of whatever Uriel was drinking.

Rum.

Not his favorite, but it would do.

"I like this one, Lucifer. You should keep her around," Uriel said, snatching her drink back and finishing it off.

"I agree," Az said, grabbing a glass from behind the bar and sliding it over to Luc. Harley poured him bourbon without being asked and handed Anna another bottle to break.

"I might have to," Luc said and took a sip of his drink. "If she breaks all my liquor, I'll have to put her to work to pay for it all."

"I'd like to see you do better." Anna stood with her hip popped out, head tilted, and the bottle in her hand. It was adorable. He wanted to lean across the bar and kiss her. Instead he took the challenge.

Luc stood, took the bottle from her hand, and expertly tossed it in the air, letting it spin a few times, then caught it, behind his back. He was showing off, but she loved it. He might need a little practice ice skating, but tossing a bottle, he could handle.

"Clearly, you've practiced," She said, taking the bottle back.

"Not recently." She didn't need to know that he'd learned that trick back in the eighties and hadn't done it since.

"Fine. I won't break any more of your stock." She put the bottle on the bar and stuck her tongue out at Luc. "Today, anyway."

"Break all you like, just use the rum and leave my bourbon alone." Luc downed the rest of his drink. "You decide what we're doing for dinner?"

"The moment I claimed the right to pick," she said,

untying the apron Harley had given her so she didn't get alcohol and glass bits on her clothes. "You ready to go?"

Luc glanced at his siblings, just to make sure there wasn't anything he needed to attend to before he agreed, then nodded. "I'm all yours."

She smiled, a mischievous little upturn in the corners of her mouth, but it spoke volumes, and Luc wanted to read them all. Harley put her hands at Anna's hips and lifted her. At the same time, she popped up, jumping onto the bar, then hopped over, landing on the floor at Luc's feet. It looked practiced, but flawless.

"Were you out here reenacting Coyote Ugly while I was in back?"

"Coyote who?" Anna tilted her head.

"Never mind. Let's go." Luc looped his arm in hers and together they walked toward the front door. "So where are we going?"

"You like tacos?" She stopped, held a finger to his lips before he could answer. "Say yes, or we can't be friends."

Friends wasn't what Luc had in mind.

"I like tacos," he said once she moved her hand and allowed him to speak. "Maybe not as fiercely as you, though."

"Okay, then we're good."

They stepped onto the sidewalk outside the club and she looked in both directions, like she wasn't sure which way to go.

"Are we walking?" Luc asked and motioned toward his car. "I can drive to this mysterious taco place."

"Okay." She shrugged. "Oh, I left my bag in your office."

"It will be fine there. We can pick it up after dinner." Luc unlocked the car and they got in. She gave him directions, or she attempted to. She wasn't completely sure where she was going since she was still relatively new to the city, but eventually, they found their way to a food truck parked near the river.

The thing was blue, with a giant clock painted on the side, with a taco in the middle. It read, *it's always time for tacos*. It looked like a million other food trucks, nothing special, but she was practically bouncing in place as they walked over.

"You really like tacos, huh?" Luc slipped his hand into hers and she practically dragged him toward the line.

"These are the best."

Once they reached the front of the line, her excitement died down a bit.

"Hey, Anna." The guy looked happy to see her, until he looked down and noticed her holding Luc's hand, then his smile faded. "What can I get ya?"

"Two specials and a couple water bottles."

"Sure thing." The guy went to fix their food and was back in no time. Luc started to pull some cash from his pocket, but she stopped him.

"My treat." She plucked a ten from her pocket and slapped it on the counter. The guy behind the counter tried to argue, but she shook her head and walked away with their meals in her hands.

"Friend of yours?" Luc asked, settling into a bench at the table she's chosen.

"Not really. His name is Sean. He screws my roommate sometimes, behind his girlfriend's back, or every time they break up. Whatever his story is anyway. I try not to pay much attention." She unwrapped the foil package to reveal two steaming tacos and her smile returned. "He's owns the truck with his brother. He's a douche, but the food is amazing."

"He has a thing for you."

"What? No," she said with her mouth full of taco. "He's just nice so I don't rat him out."

"No, that's not it." Luc shook his head. "Trust me, he's into you."

She looked behind her at Sean, who was looking in her direction, and scrunched up her nose. There was no doubt the guy liked her, but clearly no one gave him the memo that sleeping with her friends wasn't the way to a girl's heart.

"Shut up and eat your tacos." She turned back and shoved Luc's food at him.

He had to admit, they were really good tacos, but then, it had to be hard to screw up something so simple. After they finished, Luc gathered their trash and tossed it into a nearby can. She'd paid, so the least he could do was clean up the mess.

"Now what?" Anna twirled around a tree, as they walked through the park, toward the river. It was freezing out, but she didn't seem to notice. She wasn't even wearing a jacket anymore.

"We should probably get you into the car before you get frostbite." Luc pulled her against him to share his warmth.

"It's not that bad."

"It's thirty-eight degrees."

She shrugged, but snuggled against him.

"Do you want my coat? I have a suit jacket on, so I'm sure that's warmer than your sweater."

"Nah. I'll live."

He wanted to insist, to take it off himself and wrap it around her, but he held back. She was capable of knowing what she wanted and making her own decisions. And like she'd said, she would live. It didn't mean he had to like it.

"Fine, then I'll race you to the car," he said, waiting for

the coy smile to grace her lips. When it did, he released her and took off running.

"Hey, not fair," she yelled after him, running as fast as she could, but still coming in behind him. It got her to the warmth of his car faster, so he would have won either way.

Once he had her tucked inside, he blasted the heat to warm her, and she thumbed through the stations on his radio, until she found something she liked. He started driving, not really sure where they were headed, but neither seemed to mind.

This would have been the point where he suggested they go back to his place, get naked, and finish what was started back in his office earlier. But he didn't want to bring her there.

"Where to?" he asked, hoping she'd say her bed.

"The city is so beautiful at night." She sighed. "Can we just drive around a bit?"

"Sure."

And then maybe to her bed?

Luc drove her past all the usual touristy spots that the newbies to the city enjoyed. Then he took her past some of his favorite spots, letting her ask a million questions, or get out and snap a few photos here and there. The joy on her face was all he needed to make him happy.

When he ran out of things to show her, he started heading back toward the bar.

"You should probably just drop me off at home." She switched the radio station again and yawned.

"Don't you need your bag?"

"I can get it tomorrow. I won't need anything in there tonight."

"What about keys?" She didn't have a purse and Luc

doubted she had anything more than cash in her small pockets.

"My roommates should be home, if not I have a spare key outside the door."

He wanted to tell her not to tell strange men where to find her house key, that she wasn't in Kansas anymore, but he didn't. She was a big girl, who knew all those things already. At least he hoped she did, but then she did tell him, so he wasn't sure. Luc might not have any intention on hurting her, but she did just tell the devil she kept a key outside her door.

Not that she knew that.

Or not that he needed a key to get in.

Luc pulled up in front of the building she directed him to and parked the car. He wanted to walk her to the door, partly to be a gentleman, and partly because he hoped for another kiss. Apparently, it paid off, because she invited him up.

She buzzed the doorbell, and seconds later, the door swung open, and a familiar girl buzzed by.

"Can't talk, gotta go." She made a few kissing noises and hurried toward the stairs.

Anna slipped by into the apartment and motioned for Luc to join her.

"That was Destiny. She works the night shift at the diner down the street." Anna closed the door behind Luc and locked it. "She's also an actress, but her current play is for a lunch theater."

"Ambitious. Does she sleep?"

"Not enough. You want something to drink?"

He didn't. He wanted something else.

"No thank you." He took a few steps toward her and she froze. After the month he had with Talia, Luc wanted to make sure there was no questions about what she wanted. With that look on her face, he wasn't about to advance further. Even though he really wanted to strip her naked right there and take her on the coffee table. "Come here."

He waited for her to make her way over to him. She stopped a few times, as if she wasn't sure if she wanted to, or not. When she finally made it to him, she immediately slipped her hand behind his neck and pulled his mouth down to hers. Any doubt was gone. She knew exactly what she wanted and Luc was more than willing to give it to her.

He held her face with both his hands, focusing on the kiss alone. Her hand slid down from his neck and started undoing the buttons on his shirt. To make it easier for her, he loosened his tie and pulled it over his head, then tugged her sweater up, and over her head. Both were tossed to the floor, where his shirt ended up only seconds later.

"We should go to my room," She said, temporarily pulling back from his mouth. "My other roommate might be home."

Luc didn't care who was home, or who walked in. He wanted her so bad it hurt. It didn't matter what he wanted though, because she was off to her room before he could even protest. Luckily the apartment was small and he was with her, behind a closed door, in seconds flat.

Without another word, she started undoing his pants, then pushed them down to his thighs. While he got them off the rest of the way, she finished stripping down to her panties, then waited impatiently while he got the rest of his clothes off.

Once he was naked, she lunged at him, throwing herself into his arms. He stumbled back a few steps, but adjusted her, so he was supporting her with one hand, then walked her back into the wall, pressing her warm skin against the cold drywall.

She was all over him, kissing, touching, stroking. It was like a frenzy, where neither could get enough. Luc reached down and ripped her panties off, splitting the pale pink lace into pieces that hung off one leg, giving him access to the place he'd been thinking about all day.

When he slipped his hand between her thighs, letting his fingers dip into her, she groaned, and bit into his shoulder. It was all he needed to grow completely erect, maybe a bit painfully so. He ached to be inside her. It was a deep physical need that could only be satisfied by this one single woman. It wasn't anything Luc was used to, but he knew it was true. She was definitely special.

"Get on your bed." He placed her on the floor, letting the shreds of her underwear fall to her feet. She did what he said, without question, and climbed onto it backwards, never letting her eyes off of him.

When she looked down and saw the size of him, her smile grew. He was usually met with wide-eyed stares, shock, or sometimes even a bit of fear. Not Anna. She was thrilled with it.

He climbed onto the bed, slithering up between her parted legs, his eyes on hers, taking slow, deep breaths, to soak in her scent. It teased him, making his cock throb with need for her. He felt out of control, consumed by desire. All he could think of was being inside her.

Just as he was about to thrust into her, she wiggled around, flipping herself over underneath him. He dug his fingers into her round ass, kneading into the soft flesh, and spread her open for him. Then he pulled back his hips and slammed into her. She let out a scream of both pleasure and pain. It was one Luc had heard many times and it never ceased to turn him on.

"Oh my God, fuck me," she begged, with her face pressed against the flowery sheets that covered her bed.

"Leave him out of this. You're fucking the devil tonight, sweetheart," he said as he pulled back and thrust back into her, full force. Normally, he tried to ease women into it, give them a chance to adjust to his impressive size, but Anna didn't want to ease in. She wanted it as badly as he did.

Luc grabbed a handful of her hair, wrapped it around his hand, and used it to pull her neck up to his mouth. He nibbled and kissed the sensitive skin, while he slammed into her with fast repetition. With each thrust in, she screamed, loud enough for the neighbors to hear. She didn't care who heard, or how loud she was. She was lost in it, consumed the same as Luc.

She started to tighten around him, so he flipped her over, entering her from a new angle, trying to stave off her impending orgasm. He didn't want her to come, not yet anyway. He wanted to fuck her until she was sore, until she couldn't walk, until every movement she made the whole next day, was a constant reminder of how thoroughly he'd fucked her.

He pulled her legs up, wrapping her feet around his neck, so she was bent in half. It stretched her in ways he could tell she hadn't been stretched before. She groaned, and begged him not to stop, digging her nails into his biceps. He was pretty sure she was about to draw blood, but he didn't care. All he wanted was to keep pounding into her until everything around them melted away.

She angled her hips up and pressed into him so he rubbed against her clit with each thrust. Within seconds, her body squeezed around him and spasmed. She bit into his shoulder, muffling her scream, and dragged Luc into orgasm with her.

He collapsed onto his forearms, caging her body with his, pressing them together with just enough room to breathe. His face settled into her hair, and he knew right then, that if he had to pick only one woman to have sex with for the rest of his existence, this would be the one.

∽

ANNA SAT on the kitchen counter, swinging her feet, with a spoonful of peanut butter in one hand, and a cold slice of pizza in the other. She alternated bites of pizza with licks off the spoon. Georgia came in and looked at her in disgust.

"What are you pregnant?" Georgia hit the hot water button on their coffee maker and got a cup ready for tea.

Anna looked at her food choices and shrugged. "I hope not."

"Yeah well I'm pretty sure the lord heard your prayers with how loud you were screaming his name."

"That was..." She sucked the remainder of the peanut butter off the spoon and moaned. "Mmm." Then she hopped off the counter and sat in one of the chairs.

"Is he gone?" Georgia dumped some sugar into her tea and slumped into the chair across from Anna.

"Yep."

"So he just came over, screwed you, and left? And you complain about me and Sean?"

"I complain about Sean because half the time he has a girlfriend, or he's just using you when he doesn't. Come on, Georgia, he won't even let you tell anyone that you've been together. He's a creep."

"He's not a creep. He's a good guy. It's just complicated

with him and Monica. She's fragile, so he doesn't want to break it off completely yet. When she's in a better place he's gonna tell her it's over."

"That's such a load of crap."

She left out the part about seeing him, or that Luc thought he was into her. She didn't need to know either of those things.

"I know." She sighed and blew across the top of her tea. "It sounds crazy, but I believe him."

Anna shoved the cold pizza into her mouth to keep from telling Georgia she was an idiot for believing that lying asshole. It wouldn't do her any good. She wouldn't listen to Anna. She was going to believe what she wanted to believe.

"So, the new guy, was that a one time thing?"

"I really hope not, though I might have to start taking baths to soak off some of the soreness."

Georgia gave her a strange look. "How rough was he?"

"Rough, but that's not bad. He's just... huge."

"You mean, like fat?"

"No, Georgia. He's not fat." She shook her head. "His dick, *is huge*." She stressed the last part, letting it sink in.

In the few months since Anna had known Georgia, they'd never talked details about sex. Anna hadn't been getting any and Georgia was a bit shy in that department. But this time, she shocked her.

"So, how big are we talking? Like bratwurst big, or like I'm considering hiding in the corner so it can't see me, big?"

Anna spit a chunk of pizza out of her mouth and laughed. "The second one, for sure. Pretty sure I felt it in my throat when he came."

"Seriously Anna, use a condom. What are you nuts? You hardly know this guy."

"Yeah, I know. Next time." Anna smiled and thought about a repeat performance.

"Hopefully you didn't already catch chlamydia or something."

"It might have been worth it."

She knew Georgia was right, but she didn't have a condom, and there was no way she was telling him to run to the pharmacy. She could run down there in the morning herself and grab some plan b, and a box of condoms. It wasn't ideal, but it happened, so she would deal with the consequences like an adult.

And she would text him and make sure he didn't have an STD.

And then assume he would not only know for sure, but answer honestly.

For now, she would go soak her sore muscles in the tub, and hope that she could walk tomorrow to get down to the pharmacy. But damn was it worth it.

7
———

The whole way home from Anna's house, all Luc could do was think about driving right back there and throwing her back on her bed. He'd had a lot of amazing sex in his long life, but none of it felt the way it did with her. Being inside her was electric. They were like opposite poles of a magnet, being drawn together.

Was that because she was his soul mate? Or was it simply that her sin was lust and they were compatible in ways most other women couldn't even compete? He didn't feel anything that felt like what he thought love would feel like, but he'd only known her a couple days. He wasn't even sure how long it would take to know something like that.

Back in his apartment, something felt missing, empty. He wanted her there, but he couldn't risk her safety. He was kicking himself for leaving her there. He wasn't even sure why he'd left. Habit, probably, but he was definitely regretting it now.

Before he even got up to his apartment, she texted him.
'You don't have chlamydia or anything, do you?'
Then—

'We should have used a condom.'

He was about to answer and she texted again.

'OMG, you broke my twat.'

Luc laughed.

He had to admit, his dick was a bit sore as well. He could only imagine how she was feeling. Not that he would take it back if he could. He certainly wouldn't. He didn't regret fucking her hard and he didn't regret not using a condom. He didn't have to worry about catching or spreading human diseases. Angels didn't catch them. Hypothetically, he could get her pregnant, but it was a rare occurrence, and unlike human men who were fertile every moment after puberty, things worked a bit differently in angels, so he knew that hadn't happened this time.

Of course, these were things he couldn't tell her. He could say they had nothing to worry about, but she would still fear getting pregnant. Which meant she was going to make him wear one of those ridiculous cock bags.

She texted again.

With photos.

'Mmm, this bath feels nice.'

The photos showed just enough to let Luc see bits of pink skin peeking up from under bubbles, leaving him wanting more. It was almost enough to make him say screw it and rush back over there. Then she sent one more photo, a little more revealing, with half of her breast and a hand covering the good parts. It was enough to make up his mind and have him turning back around. That was until he heard his brother behind him in the dark.

"What are you laughing at?" Gabriel turned on the lamp in the apartment from where he sat in Luc's favorite chair. Why did they always pick his favorite chair?

"Brother, you're here earlier than expected." Luc shoved

his phone into his pocket and went to pour a drink. He had a feeling he was going to need it. Dealing with Gabriel was never a good time.

"And you're off fooling around, instead of guarding the tablet, I see."

"The tablet is safe." Luc drank half a glass of bourbon, then poured another. "Did you expect me to be sitting in front of it around the clock until Michael decided to show up?"

"Maybe you should be."

"He didn't show up, so it all worked out."

"The pull in here is strong." Gabriel stood up and closed his eyes for a long moment. "My connection with Michael lets me feel it."

"It's also what makes me wonder if I should be trusting you." Luc finished the second drink, poured a third, and took a seat on the couch.

"Good. I would be disappointed if you trusted me without reason, Lucifer." Gabriel walked over to the bar, poured himself a drink, and returned to the chair. "However, I intend to give you reason. I'm not happy with our brother for his current behavior, and like you, don't wish to see the humans destroyed."

"I'm glad to hear that."

"I spoke with Michael."

"Oh?" Luc raised his brow and leaned forward. "And what did he have to say?"

"He's out of his mind. I'm not sure he's even recognizable any longer." Gabriel sipped his drink and frowned. "He wants to destroy the humans, wipe the slate clean. Start over."

That's what Luc was afraid of. There was no way he could let Michael win with those intentions.

"Why?" It was the one question Luc had wondered since the beginning and the one that he wanted answered most of all.

"He believes that Father made a mistake in giving them so much freedom, and that by doing so, they have destroyed the planet. He's taken it upon himself to use the demons to get rid of them, then he plans on destroying them as well."

"When did Michael stop caring about Father's rules?"

"I'm not sure he has."

"Father doesn't want this, Gabriel. I spoke with him about it."

"True, but Michael has taken things Father has said, and twisted them. He believes that what he's doing truly is Father's will."

"Like he did when he banished me from our home?" Luc shook his head.

"Like that, only worse, because he isn't right in the head. Something is definitely wrong with him. I explained that Father didn't want him to have, or use, the Hell Tablet. And that he certainly didn't want any harm to come to the humans, but he wasn't hearing me."

"Did you explain that if he pursued this, you would fight by my side?" Luc hoped that was actually Gabe's intention.

"I did and he found it amusing. Honestly, I don't think he believed me." Gabriel took another sip of his drink and looked at the liquid in the glass like he was surprised by it.

"You think you will have no trouble choosing sides against Michael?"

"I'll admit, it wasn't an easy decision to go against him. We've always been close. Fighting Michael, would be like fighting myself. I will take no part in killing him, but I understand that you have to protect the tablet."

"I have no intention of killing my brother." Luc sat back and stared at Gabe. "Do you really think so little of me?"

"Let's be honest, Lucifer, I hardly know you. We might be siblings, but we were never close. Besides, I haven't seen you in thousands of years."

"I suppose that's fair."

"What do you plan to do with him then? He won't surrender."

"I plan to put him in the Hell Box and lock him up until a better solution is brought to light."

"I suppose that's a good plan. He'll be here soon. You should prepare yourself." Gabriel put the glass on the coffee table and crossed his legs at the ankles. "I'll be staying until then."

"When you say soon...?"

"My guess would be by the end of the week. Maybe sooner. I've already spoken to Uriel and Azrael. Oh and your little demon pet was there, so she knows too."

"She isn't my pet."

"Whatever. I'm tired. I'll take your bed." Gabriel got up and went to make himself comfortable in Luc's bed.

Luc hoped Michael would get there sooner, rather than later. If for no other reason, than to get rid of Gabriel. He wasn't sure he could take almost a week of him.

∼

SHE'D TEXTED him four times, with *almost* dirty photos, and he hadn't responded. What did that even mean? Maybe he wasn't that into her. Except that it hadn't felt like that at all when they were together. But then they'd slept together, not that there was any sleeping involved, and now he was radio silent.

Anna rolled out of bed and groaned. Everything hurt. Well, not everything, but all the important places. The pathetic part was, if he showed up in her bedroom right that moment, she'd strip naked and let him split her open all over again. It was just that good.

Now she had to find a way to get dressed and drag herself over to his club to follow him around all day again. After they'd had sex and he'd ignored her. This is what she got for lecturing Georgia about Sean. It was her punishment.

She hobbled into the bathroom to pee and found a post-it note on her mirror, saying *don't forget the plan b you dirty whore*. It was from Destiny, who shouldn't know she slept with Luc. So clearly, Georgia had a big mouth. Which was probably a good thing, because she would have forgotten.

Though, she did have a few days to take it. Maybe she should wait and roll the dice a few more times. Well, that is if he was still interested. Since he wasn't answering her texts, maybe she should assume he wasn't.

Anna took a quick shower, threw on some comfortable clothes, and towel dried her hair the best she could. She grabbed a bagel and headed out the door. After stopping at the pharmacy, she hurried to the club to follow Luc around for another day. And of course, to see why he hadn't answered her texts.

She wasn't going to ask him. At least that's what she was telling herself. As she saw him walking over, she started to lose her confidence.

"Hey," she said, trying to sound casual.

He smiled immediately, sweeping her into his arms and kissing her, like it was the most natural thing to do. That was definitely not what she was expecting, but she was more than happy to roll with it. She certainly wasn't turning it down. Even if she probably had bagel breath.

"That's some hello," she said when he finally released her, a little more breathless than when he'd started.

"It was the best I could do on short notice. What's in the bag?" He stuck a finger in the top before she could stop him and peeked inside. "Plan b?"

"It's ya know, to make sure we didn't accidentally make some little Lucifers last night." She pulled the bag back and crumbled down the top. The last thing she needed to do was explain her purchase to his siblings, or best friend.

"You won't need that."

"Why? Are you sterile or something?"

"Of course not. Not normally."

"What does that mean?"

"It means I'm one hundred percent sure I didn't get you pregnant, so don't suffer through that awful thing. Also, I'm sorry I didn't answer your texts last night. I was just about to respond when my brother Gabriel showed up."

Well that made sense, because after that kiss, she was sure he was still interested.

"Oh, and don't worry, I didn't give you any diseases either." Luc chuckled and led her toward his office.

"How can you be sure about that? I'm sure you've had sex with other women recently, so you can't know who they've been with. It's the whole, you're sleeping with the people your partner has slept with thing."

"I'm not sure what that thing is, but I assure you, I'm clean. However, I can understand why you don't trust me. It's a safe practice. And I noticed the condoms you bought." Luc smiled, holding open the office door for her to go in first. "I'm not sure they'll fit, but we can try."

"Haven't you used condoms before?"

"Actually, no. A few women have requested it, but I've never found one that will cover me without breaking."

"That doesn't make me feel better to know every time you've had sex, it was unprotected."

Luc frowned. "I'd be happy to get tested, if it would make you feel better."

"Actually, it would."

To be honest, if he wanted to bend her over the couch right there in his office, she wouldn't have said no. But at least this way she would know.

"Aren't you concerned about what you might catch from *me*?" she asked, taking a seat with him on the couch.

"Not at all."

"Why not?"

"I have a strong immune system. Now the sweatpants are cute, but take them off, and sit in my lap."

He was so causal about the whole thing she almost didn't realize what he'd said. He laughed at her when the realization clicked and her eyes widened. She was still sore from last night, so sore that it was uncomfortable just sitting there, but she was up and stripping before her body could protest.

Luc undid his pants and slid them down before she managed to get her bottom half naked. She ignored the rest and climbed in his lap. She thought about trying the condom on him, just to see, but looked down, and realized he was probably right.

That pivotal moment, she could have turned back, said no without the protection, but she didn't. She was all in. He pulled her shirt over her head and nuzzled his face into her bra. As nice as it felt, she wanted him against her skin, so she reached behind her, unclasped the bra, and tossed it on the floor with the rest of her clothes.

Immediately, he went to work on her nipples, catching one between his teeth and sucking it into his mouth. That was all it took to have her dripping onto his cock, completely ready for him.

She rocked herself against him, creating a sweet friction along her clit. He put his hands on her hips, helping her move against him, making sure she slid high enough to thump the head of his cock against her each time.

He switched to her other nipple just when the first got too sensitive and went about biting, licking, and sucking that one until she thought she might scream. His tongue was amazing, his skill perfect. She could only imagine what he could do with it down a bit lower. As much as she wanted to find out, she wanted him inside her more.

She ached for it, shivered with the anticipation. She tried to wriggle herself into position, but he pulled her back, keeping her just out of reach from where she needed him. Frustrated, she grabbed his face in her hands and pulled it up to look at her.

"I need you inside me, Luc."

He smiled and shook his head. "Not yet."

"Yes, now." She was breathless, practically panting with need for him, still rocking against him, bringing herself closer to orgasm before he even got inside her.

"I want you to come for me first." He nipped at her nipple, without breaking eye contact.

"Fuck me and I will."

"Come for me and I'll fuck you."

It was the way he said it, the sound of his voice, raw, almost a growl. It had her head thrown back, and coming, as if she could do it on demand. Before she could catch her breath, he pushed her back, positioned himself, and thrust inside her in one slow motion. He didn't go all the way in and she was grateful for it. He continued his slow, delicious, assault on her body, easing further in each time, until she could handle most of him.

In the daylight, she wondered how she ever fit all of him inside her last night, or how she took as much as she did now. It would be a lie to say it didn't hurt, but at the same time, it felt too divine to stop.

Luc grabbed a handful of her hair, pulled her head back to expose her neck, and nibbled at the sensitive skin there. His other hand stayed at her hip, directing their motion, setting the pace. He intentionally forced them into a slow rhythm, even when she tried to speed him up. He held her back, kept her from being too rough. She could tell it was a struggle for him, that he was likely doing it to keep from hurting her too much.

But that ship had sailed and she didn't care.

She could take a three hour bath, or sleep with a hot water bottle between her legs, or she could pop a handful of ibuprofen. Whatever it took to keep enjoying the feel of him inside her, she would do. How was she supposed to walk away from this at the end of the week?

The veins at Luc's temples pulsed and he strained to hold on. He needed release and she understood that desperate attempt to hold on to control that she saw in his eyes.

"Your turn," she whispered against his ear, biting the lobe before moving back.

"After you, love," he growled, fighting to keep their slow pace.

She pushed his hand off her hip and took control of their speed, sliding herself back and forth as fast as she could physically go. He didn't try to stop her this time.

Instead, he let his hands drop to his sides, and came along for the ride.

Almost immediately, she felt herself start to build again, tightening around him, making the snug fit even tighter. Luc groaned and closed his eyes. A few seconds later, and she was screaming her second orgasm of the morning into his hair, as he pressed her against him, taking the last of what he needed to follow.

Anna was spent, her body too sore and used up, to move. She laid against Luc, panting into his neck, with his arms wrapped tight around her. It was all she could do to breathe. Not even when she heard the knock at the door, or when it creaked open, then slammed shut, did she move. She didn't even care, who it was, or that it happened. She never wanted to move.

Luc didn't rush her. He stayed in the same position, just breathing with her, for a long time. After that, he combed his fingers through her hair, separating the tangled strands, section by section. Eventually, he started to scratch her back, soothing her into sleep. And even then, he didn't try to move her. He let her doze in his lap until she was able to finally keep her eyes open and move.

She felt a little guilty keeping him trapped there so long, but his smile told her he hadn't minded. As soon as he was free, he put on his pants, and got her a water bottle. Her crumpled brown paper bag with the plan b and condoms sat on the floor with her clothes. The clothes he picked up and placed on the couch next to her. If he'd been rushing her, he would have handed them to her, but he didn't. He picked the bag up and put it on his desk.

"Are you worried I gave you chlamydia still?" Luc leaned against the desk with his too-damn-sexy half smile.

"Maybe, but I'm going to die here anyway, so it won't matter."

"I might have to carry you around for the next day or two, or four, since I will definitely not be letting you rest that much."

"Are you saying you haven't gotten enough, you insatiable pig?" she asked, slipping her bra back on and pulling her shirt over her head.

"Not even close."

How much she wanted him, even then, when she could hardly dress herself from exhaustion, and feeling like she'd just screwed a horse, was mind blowing. She was really hoping he didn't suggest they go again, because she wasn't positive she could say no.

He was like crack and she couldn't get enough.

This article might just be the death of her.

But she sure was going to go out with a bang.

~

Luc left Anna in his office to nap, with Jason and one of the new demon guards outside to make sure she was safe. Technically, the office was protected with the club, but he wasn't taking any chances with her. The poor thing was exhausted and walking like she'd been riding a horse, bareback, for three days straight. He felt guilty about it, but not enough to stop from wanting her again.

Not that he would tell Harley, but he did cheat a little and use his power to take away most of her soreness. He left just enough so she would know how well she'd been fucked. He was a good guy like that.

At the very least though, he would let her rest while he did some work and checked in on how things were going.

The last thing he wanted to hear was Gabriel lecturing him about how he needed to be there with the tablet, ready for Michael to show up at any moment.

It wasn't that he was wrong. Luc did need to be prepared for the eventual fight that was getting closer by the day. But he also had to live his life. He had other responsibilities that couldn't be ignored, and well, he had Anna.

At least for the month.

Even just a few days in, he was already thinking about how he was going to be away from her. If she *was* the right one, he'd promised to stick it out for the whole seven sins. That left two more to get through before he could be with any of the girls. It seemed like an impossible situation. He had been worried that he wouldn't find his true love by the end of the game, now he was worried that he would, and he would have to say goodbye while he spent time with two more girls.

"Is it true?" Gabriel appeared behind Luc and put his hand on Luc's shoulder.

"Is what true?" Luc shrugged his brother off and sat at the bar. Harley was off doing something on the other side, so he grabbed a glass and poured himself a bourbon.

"That you're intentionally bringing human females into your life when Michael is looking for reasons to bring you down?"

Luc shook his head and sighed. He didn't want to have this conversation with Gabe. It was none of his business.

"I'm trying to find a mate. Surely even I deserve that?"

"Not if it's going to get her killed." Gabe reached behind the bar and grabbed the whiskey and a glass.

"I'm doing my best to protect her. It's not like I'm going out of my way to dangle her in front of Michael."

"She still goes home, unprotected. If he wanted to get to

you, that would be one way. It's what I would do." Gabe poured a full glass of whiskey and drank it down in one go.

"That's good to know, Gabe, and maybe if I was in love with her, that would make sense. But I just met this girl. I can't protect every woman I might enjoy, twenty-four seven. Michael has better things to do with his time."

Gabe poured another glass and drank it down too. The guy was worse than Az. Luc was going to have to order more whiskey before this week was up.

"What happens when you do fall in love with her? Or with a different one?"

"I'm hoping that this will be done by then and Michael will be securely locked away."

"And the next enemy?"

"What are you saying? I shouldn't find love because people may hold a grudge against me? I never asked for any of this. It wasn't my idea to have me in charge of Hell, or the tablet. You know damn well that Father would have gotten over his anger with me and things would have been fine. That was all Michael then. It's all him now. Why am I always the one paying the price?"

Gabriel put his arm around Luc and pulled him against his side. It was an awkward show of brotherly love, but Luc wasn't thrilled with it.

"I am sorry, brother. I never agreed with what Michael did. I supported him because of our relationship, but I know it was wrong. I would probably be supporting him now, if he wasn't so far lost. His actions back then condemned you to this fate, and that wasn't right. But his actions now may condemn billions and I can't stand behind that."

"I'm not really sure how to take that." Luc shrugged Gabe off and finished off his drink. "But I'm glad to have you on my side this time."

8

Anna woke up and stretched. She looked around to get her bearings. The room was dark and she wondered just how long she'd slept. Too long obviously. She had work to do. She wasn't there for amazing sex, day drinking, and naps. She had an article to write, and to do that, she needed to follow through. This opportunity was too important to waste it with momentary pleasure.

Even if that pleasure was astounding.

Luc had covered her with a blanket and left her a note saying he'd be around the club doing work. He was thoughtful. She had to give him that.

She slipped her shoes back on and drank down half the water he'd left her with, then went to find him. Hopefully he was still doing work, so she could salvage at least an hour or two for the day. She crept by a couple security guards in the hall and made her way out to the main area of the place. The club was already getting busy and she had to wander around a bit to find him.

Luc was in a corner, arguing with some guy. It was calm and civil, but she could feel his irritation from there. The connection she felt with him wasn't anything she ever felt before. It was like they shared some energy, and it allowed her to feel him, for lack of better words.

Not that she planned on mentioning that to him.

It would make her sound like a nut job.

She waited a moment, then walked over. Both men stopped talking the instant they noticed her.

"Annalee, I see you've woken up. You look refreshed." Luc welcomed her in and put his arm around her. "This is my brother, Gabriel. Gabe, this is Anna."

Gabe nodded. "Nice to meet you, Anna. I hope someone has warned you about this devil."

"I can't imagine anything I'd need to be warned about. Luc is one of the sweetest guys I've met since I moved here."

Gabe laughed. "That's... well, I'm glad you two are hitting it off. Sometime soon, we should all get together, have dinner or something. Lucifer is an excellent cook."

Luc shot his brother an odd look, then nodded. "I am, and we should. Maybe in a couple weeks."

"Good. Then I'll be off." Gabe bowed his head at Anna and walked off.

"Everything okay?" she asked Luc, shrugging out from under his arm to face him.

"Of course. Why wouldn't it be okay?"

"It looked like you two were arguing."

"Just sibling stuff. Nothing you need to worry about. Feeling better?"

"Actually, yeah, quite a bit. Sorry I flaked on you and fell asleep. I'm not doing a very professional job here, am I?"

"Oh, I'd say you were doing an excellent job, but I do apologize. I know you have a story to write and I didn't do much to help that."

"I'd say we can share the blame on that."

"There's a show here tonight, magic I think. Why don't you see if your roommates are free and you can all come enjoy it? It will give you more of an idea what goes on around here, and if you want, you can follow me around on anything important. Or you can just enjoy the show with your friends. Whichever you like."

"That sounds great. I know Destiny is actually off tonight, so as long as Georgia is up for it, we'll probably be there."

"Perfect. Why don't you take off and see to that then. I think it's time for me to take a nap of my own."

She almost wanted to suggest she go with him, help tire him out some more, but she wanted to make sure she could walk tonight. She actually felt better than she expected, but there was only so many times she could push her luck and have it work out in her favor. Sex with Luc was already the universe smiling down on her. She just didn't have that much karma racked up.

"Okay, get some rest," she said. "But later..." She winked and spun around to leave. Before she could get away, he grabbed her arm, pulled her against him, and kissed her with everything he had. It left her wobbly on her feet and he kept his hands on her hips to steady her.

"I'm gonna hold you to that," he said, then let her go and walked toward the back stairs.

"Be careful what you wish for, Anna," she said out loud to her self.

You just might get it.

LUC COULDN'T SLEEP. He tried, but Gabe's words kept playing over in his mind. It didn't help that the asshole also wanted a nap and was peacefully sleeping in Luc's bed, while Luc was scrunched onto his sofa. So after laying there for an hour, doing nothing more than rethinking all the decisions he'd made over the last several months, he got up, and decided to go see Cupid.

It probably wasn't the best idea, but he had to try.

As soon as he walked in the warehouse that the group of mages he'd worked with called home, he could feel the chatter. He might not be able to actually decipher their thoughts, the way he could with humans, but he could pick up on the bits and pieces that came through as a jumbled mess.

Oz walked out and met him before he got halfway through the room. "Lucifer, nice to see you. Is there something I can do for you?"

Luc didn't expect him to just allow him to wander freely, but he gave off a vibe that he was hiding something. Then again, the mages often did. It was one of the reasons most others didn't trust them, whether it was justified, or not.

"I'd like to see Cupid."

Oz nodded and led him in back where they kept prisoners. They had to walk past Aivah, the mage that Luc slept with before having brought there. She had done the right thing in the end and helped them, but she was still holding a grudge, evidenced by the glares she was giving him. It was probably a very good thing that she couldn't use any magic in there.

Cupid was in a corner, reading a book, like nothing was wrong in the world. He looked up and smiled when he saw Luc. "Hello, cousin. How are things?"

"Adapting to the situation as usual, I see." Luc pulled over a chair and took a seat outside the cage.

"You know me." Cupid put the book down and walked to the bars to stand in front of Luc.

"I thought I did," Luc said and Cupid frowned.

"I never wanted things to turn out the way they did. I am sorry for that."

"Instead, you would have rather carried out your own plan to '*take me down a notch*' I'm pretty sure were your exact words?"

"I was angry, and it was wrong, I know that. But we are where we are. It's where we go from here that matters. Don't you think?"

"You sound like a fortune cookie." Luc rolled his eyes and crossed one leg over the other.

"I'm sitting behind bars, so I have the time to be insightful."

"How are you liking it in there anyway?" Luc glanced at his watch and looked around, avoiding making eye contact with Cupid.

"The mages can snap up any food they want. As far as prisons go, this one isn't half bad."

"That's because I haven't decided what to do with you yet. Once I do, things will be quite different for you."

"Don't hold a grudge, Lucifer. There was once a time you were the outcast."

"Because I challenged my father's rules, not because I actively tried to help destroy the world and an entire species."

"To be fair, I didn't know what I was getting myself into."

"I'm not in the mood to be fair, Cupid. Sit down and shut up."

Cupid did as Luc said.

"You've had some time here to think about your part in

all of this. Have you thought of anything that might assist us in taking my psychopath brother down?"

Cupid was quiet for a long while. Luc was patient. He would wait it out because he could tell Cupid was wrestling with something on a deep level. When he made his decision, Luc was ready to hear it.

"There might be something, but it's not anything I'm comfortable being a part of."

"How comfortable are you with the idea of finding yourself in one of these cages, down in Hell?"

Cupid sighed dramatically, then tossed his blond hair behind him. "Fine, but I need you to promise me you won't hurt her."

"I'll need to know what you're talking about first."

"Michael has a mate."

Luc stood up and squared his shoulders. This was the first he'd heard of any such thing. He didn't even think Michael was interested in that sort of thing.

"Human?"

Cupid nodded, but kept his head turned away. "He plans to kill her, send her to heaven himself, then bring her back after the world is barren, to start over. Like they're some sort of second wave Adam and Eve."

"And she's okay with that?"

"To be honest, I'm not sure she knows what his plans are. I can't even be sure she's a willing participant in the relationship."

"What does that mean?" Luc reached through the bars and grabbed Cupid by his shirt.

"I got the impression that he was using angel powers on her, or maybe even magic, or both. Love is what I do, regardless of what you think of me, and I didn't feel that there. Not from her."

"You actually met her?" Luc loosened his grip on Cupid, but didn't let go.

"He originally came to me to make her fall in love. I explained I couldn't do that."

"Isn't that exactly what you do?"

"No." Cupid yanked free of Luc. "I help compatible people find one another. I nudge, but I don't force people to love one another. That's just rude, Lucifer."

"Whatever. So when you wouldn't help?"

"It's not that I wouldn't, but I wouldn't even if I could. It's that I couldn't. He was angry, but he didn't bring it up again. The next time I saw her, they were *in love*. I didn't mention it."

"And you think this helps me how?"

"What do you think Michael would do if you found your soul mate right now? Don't you think he would use her to get the tablet?"

Of course he would. Luc already knew Michael would stoop to that level, but did he want to do what Michael would do?

"Look," Cupid said. "I'm not saying to hurt her. You don't have to be a crazy monster like your brother. But if you were to somehow acquire her—"

"She's a person, Cupid. Not an object. She shouldn't be used that way."

"No, she shouldn't, but if Michael somehow forced her to think she's in love with him, wouldn't it be better to get her away from him? He doesn't have pure motives for her either."

"He is definitely planning on using the tablet. He told Gabriel he was."

"I figured as much. You have to stop him, Lucifer."

"What's her name?"

"Melanie."

Luc paced the area in front of the cells. He didn't want to hurt anyone. He didn't want to tear apart Michael from his mate, if she might possibly really be that. But once he locked Michael up, they would be parted anyway. How would that be any better than what his father wanted to do to him?

"Are you positive that she's not his true love?"

"Not one hundred percent. If you can get her away from him, find out if she's been compelled, or had magic used on her, then I can let you know. I know it's pointless to ask you to trust me, but trust me. You know I don't want this world destroyed. This is my home, too."

There was no benefit to Cupid to lie about any of this. Luc knew Cupid wouldn't want the tablet used. He did believe that the idiot didn't know what he was doing when he got involved, but that didn't mean he trusted him. But something had to be done. He needed this whole thing over with. He had to get Michael in that box so he could not only keep all of humanity safe, but so he could make sure the people he cared about were safe.

And right now, the top priority was Anna.

∽

"THIS PLACE IS HOT." Georgia spun around between her roommates and looked around.

"So is the owner." Destiny elbowed Anna and yanked both girls toward the bar. "Where is he anyway? Tell me he's going to make an appearance?"

Anna was sure he would, but she didn't want to share him with the girls. She almost wished she hadn't brought them, just so she could keep that one thing all to herself.

"I'm sure he has work to do." She shrugged. "Maybe you'll see him later." Anna squeezed between some people and got Harley's attention.

"Hey Annalee. What can I get for you?" Harley waved some guys away to make more room for Anna and her friends.

"I'll have a tequila and ginger ale." Anna turned to her friends.

"Oh me too," Georgia said, practically bouncing in place.

"Beer," Destiny said and reached into her purse for some money.

"Keep it honey, it's on the house." Harley went about making the drinks and seconds later, had a glass thrust at each of them.

"Thanks." Destiny winked and giggled. Anna wanted to push her aside and stop her from embarrassing herself.

Georgia took the drink without a sound and immediately started sucking it down. They were probably going to be tucking her drunk ass into bed before the night was over.

"Thanks for the drinks," Anna said to Harley when she handed her the drink.

"You don't pay here. That's Luc, not me. He should be around in a bit, by the way."

Anna nodded. She didn't get the impression Harley would charge her either way. She was always looking at her in strange ways. Anna didn't know what to make of it.

"Hey," Harley called out and grabbed Anna's arm before she could get away. "Luc has you set up in the VIP section. You guys can go get comfortable. There's a girl up there that will get you whatever you need."

There was no girl that could get Anna what she needed. What she needed was some more alone time with Luc.

Hopefully she could get him up to his apartment before the night was up.

Anna led her friends over to the VIP section and they were shown to a table reserved just for them. Their names were written on a card in fancy script that Georgia just had to take photos of to post online.

"This is awesome." Destiny flopped down on the velvet seat. "Can you keep screwing this guy so we can always come here?"

"Seriously, Des?" Georgia glared at their friend. "Don't embarrass her."

"What? I'm not embarrassing her. No one can even hear me."

A guy in the next table was smiling at Anna. It was one of those creepy smiles that said, *if you're fucking him, can you do me too*? He definitely heard Destiny.

"When does the show start?" Georgia looked around, snapping photos at every angle.

"At ten I think, so we have some time. We can—"

"Ladies," Luc said, appearing in front of them. "Glad you could make it. I hope you're enjoying yourselves."

"It's incredible." Destiny popped up and grabbed Luc's hand, forcing him into a handshake. "We met in the hall."

Anna rolled her eyes.

"Uh, yeah. I remember." Luc smiled. "Actress slash waitress."

"You should come see the show when it opens. It's nothing like this place, but you might like it."

"Sit down Destiny," Georgia said, pulling at Destiny's skirt. "You're gonna get drool on his expensive suit."

Luc stifled a laugh and leaned in to kiss Anna once Destiny let him go.

"Hello beautiful," he said just loud enough for her

friends to overhear. "I'm really glad you came." Then he leaned in and whispered in her ear. "And I can't wait to make you come. Again."

"I can't wait either." Anna dragged her eyes down him, making sure he knew where her eyes most wanted to settle.

"Would you like to shadow me while I go check on things for the show?"

"I would—" Destiny started saying and Georgia kicked her.

"Yes, of course." Luc extended a hand to Anna and she took it, jumping to her feet. "I'll be back."

"I'll return her to you before the show starts. Just let Alexis know if you ladies need anything." Luc motioned in the direction of the supermodel that led them to their seats and whisked Anna away.

She followed him behind the stage area and watched as he checked in on the magician and any staff that was working back there. It only took about fifteen minutes, but it was one more thing she could use when she finally sat down to write her article on him.

After he finished, he walked her over to a dark dressing room, and led her inside. Without a word, or turning on a light, he pushed her against the door, and kissed her savagely. It was the raw, nothing-but-need, kind of kiss, that told of more to come.

"I was thinking about you," he said once they pulled back to breathe.

"Oh yeah?"

"Yes."

"What about me?"

"Kissing you." He leaned in and kissed her again.

"And biting you." He leaned in once more and nipped at her neck.

"And touching you." He ran his hands down her body until he came to the hem of her skirt, then slipped under it, reaching into her panties, then dipped one finger into her, and coated it with her juices.

"And tasting you." He brought his finger up to his mouth and licked her off of him. "Mmm." He kissed her again, sharing her taste with her. "I can't wait to press my face between your thighs and lick every bit of you." His voice was low, gravely, and it made her insane with need.

"What's stopping you?" She was ready to push his face down there right now. Hell, with how much she wanted him, they could have done it right on the stage, and she wouldn't have cared.

"You're a very bad girl."

"Isn't that what you like about me?"

"It's definitely one of the things."

The ache in her middle was so strong she had to clamp her legs together to ease it back. "So... if you missed all those things, and we're here in this dark room all alone..."

"The show is gonna start soon and I promised your friends I'd have you back to them."

"Who cares? Fuck me."

He was still for a moment, and she couldn't tell what he was doing, because it was too dark. Then she felt him, he slipped her underwear down her legs and let them drop to her feet. He lifted one leg, and pulled them off that side, letting them dangle off the other. Then he took her leg and propped it up on his shoulder. He must have been kneeling, or something like that, because she could feel his breath right between her legs.

Nothing happened for an eternity, which was probably only about thirty seconds, but with his hot breath hitting her skin, so close to the place she wanted him most, even five seconds was too long.

She started reaching out and found his head. She was just about to push his face toward her, when he stuck his tongue into her. It was like immediate heaven. The wet, hot, flicks of his tongue against her clit, had her panting and clutching his hair to hold on. It was sure to be the fastest orgasm of her life.

"Oh fuck," she hissed. "Slow down."

Luc shook his head, side to side, without stopping his incessant licking, sucking, and flicking. It was intense. It made her see stars. It had her sliding to the floor, screaming out his name. Luc caught her by the ass, keeping her from actually making it all the way down, as she shook and twitched, with the last spasms of orgasm, half squatting against the wall.

He took a deep breath in of her and said, "damn, you're amazing."

"Me?" She shook her head in the dark. "You're the one who's amazing. That was all you, babe." She reached out for him, but he stood, just out of her reach. As if he had the vision of a cat, he grabbed her hand and pulled her to her feet.

"We should go."

"But—"

He covered her lips with his, mixing her taste between their mouths. His body was pressed against her, leaving no doubt that he was ready for more, but he adjusted himself, and cracked the door open for light.

"Let's go."

He shoved her panties into her hand, that had somehow gotten off her other leg, and pulled her into the harsh light of the hallway. Several security guards nodded and smiled as they passed, letting her know they knew exactly what was going on just seconds earlier. Anyone who got close to Luc would know as well, since his face smelled of her scent.

"What am I supposed to do with these?" She tried to hand the underwear back to him, shove them into his pocket, anything but stand there and hold them crumpled into her fist.

"I thought you might want to put them back on, but if not, that's fine too."

She stood there, nearly in sight of her friends, holding her underwear in her hand, trying to decide right then if she wanted to go put them on in the bathroom, or insist he hold onto them. Before she could decide, Luc snatched them out of her hand, held them up to his face, and took a deep breath in.

"On second thought, I think I'll hold on to them."

Before she could protest, he was walking over to her roommates.

"See, I have her back right before the show is about to start. You ladies can either stay here and watch, or you can move up to the table right in front. There's a card reserving it for you, if you choose." Luc smiled at her friends, playing the perfect host, while she slipped into the cushioned seat, hoping they wanted to stay where they were. At least then, she felt less on display.

Thankfully, they agreed they wanted to stay in the VIP section. It seemed fancier to them and Anna let out a relieved sigh. Before walking away, Luc leaned in and whispered into her ear once more.

"Stop by my office before you leave. I want to be dripping out of your pussy the whole way home." He pulled back, bit her bottom lip, and left her there with Destiny and Georgia staring at her.

"What was that about?" Georgia narrowed her eyes.

"He was thanking her for the quickie in the bathroom." Destiny elbowed her hard in the ribs. "He was, wasn't he?"

"There was no quickie in the bathroom." Anna held one finger up to her lips and pointed toward the stage.

They left her alone to watch the show, which was spectacular. Not that she'd expected less from Luc, or his club. She didn't need a week to learn that he was serious about his business and that nothing that happened there would be disappointing.

Especially not getting oral sex in a dark dressing room.

After the show, the girls insisted on having more drinks, and dancing. Anna took the opportunity to text Luc and tell him they'd be leaving soon. As expected, he told her to meet him in his office, and she snuck away to meet him.

He was standing in the middle of the room when she walked in, his pants already undone. Just looking at him got her wet. She had always been a sexual person, but no guy had ever made her feel that constant need, the way Luc did. She couldn't get enough of him, and from the way his pants bulged, he felt the same.

Again, without a word, he pulled her into the room, pushed her over the arm of the couch, and slammed his dick inside her from behind. It was one quick thrust, that filled her completely. He wrapped his hand around her hair with one hand, and dug his fingers into her ass with the other. Between the two, he pulled out and pushed back, falling into a hard, fast rhythm, that slammed her into the couch with enough force to make it jump.

It was exactly what she needed, as if he could read her mind, and give her what she wanted, when she wanted it, perfectly how she needed it. He was like some sort of sex god.

He pulled her hair back harder, lifting her up, and kissed her neck. The combination of hard fucking, with gentle kisses, had her lost in sensory overload. Her head spun and she wasn't even sure if she was breathing at that point. The world blurred around her.

At some point, she was pretty sure she could hear herself cry out, but it sounded far away. With it, came an intense pleasure, as all the sensations her body took in, came together in one point, stabbing through her, and spreading over her body in waves.

She closed her eyes for a long moment. When she opened them, Luc was holding her in his arms, stroking her hair back away from her face. There was something so calming about it, so safe, that she never wanted it to end.

It was like an out of body experience. The whole thing probably took less than ten minutes, but it felt like hours had passed, like time was winding down slowly, and minutes existed between each tick of the clock. It was unreal.

"Your friends are texting you," Luc whispered, handing her phone to her.

Anna took it, but ignored the texts. They could wait a few minutes.

"I need more for my story."

"Sex? You little minx."

"Not sex." She slapped him. "Work. As much as I love this." And she did love it. "I have to write an amazing article. My career depends on it."

"I can't get enough of you." Luc slipped one hand under her shirt and pinched one nipple between his fingers, then rolled it, making her clench her teeth, and push him off to get her thoughts back.

"Well, no more, until I get enough for my story." She

totally didn't mean it. If he wanted to go again right then, she would have been all for it. But she wanted to mean it, so she hoped that he would at least think she did.

"Fine," he said. "Tomorrow, I will show you all the things." Luc circled his finger in her public hair. "Oh, you want these back?" He held up her underwear and she reached for them. "On second thought, I'll give them back tomorrow. I like the idea of your bare ass, on my leather car seat, dripping my come down your thighs."

"Are you driving me home?"

"Jason will. I have a few things to take care of with my family. If that's okay?"

"Sure." She nodded.

With that, Luc was up and helping her to her feet. She adjusted her clothes the best she could, smoothed her hand over her hair, and went to find her friends. They would know exactly what was going on and she didn't care.

She wouldn't change a single thing about this night.

9

"So Q thinks that this Melanie chick is being compelled to be Michael's mate?" Az handed out drinks to Uriel and Gabriel, then took a seat on the couch.

"Don't call him that," Luc said. "He's a big enough douche. But yes. He said he picked up on magic, too."

"Why does he think she's not really in love with him?" Uriel sipped her drink and placed it on the coffee table. "I mean, our kind is quite appealing to humans. It doesn't seem unreasonable that she might fall in love with him. Maybe she doesn't know what a psychopath he is?"

"Cupid just knows these things, I guess. He said the first time he met her, there were no indications of love. Also, Michael wanted him to force her into loving him, or some shit like that."

"And Cupid told him no?" Gabriel raised his brow and gulped down half his drink. "Then lived to tell the tale?"

"Not exactly." Luc paced the room, restless. "Apparently, Cupid doesn't force love on humans. He nurtures feelings that are already possible. It has to be the right pairing, or some shit like that. If they aren't compatible, then he can't do anything to make it work. So Michael wasn't happy, but there was nothing Cupid could do about it. The next time he saw them, they were in love, or whatever."

"So," Uriel said. "He's using a mage to reinforce what he compelled from her."

"It's possible." Gabe gulped down the rest of his drink and held the glass out to Az. Az stared at him for a long moment, sighed, then got up to pour more.

"That's disgusting." Uriel waved a hand in the air and crossed and recrossed her legs. "Just thinking about it makes my skin crawl. What kind of angel needs to compel human affections?"

"One who's fucked in the head, like our brother." Az handed Gabe the drink, filled to the top of the glass, and put the bottle on the table in front of him.

"So what do you want to do, Lucifer?" Gabe asked. "You want to take this woman? And do what with her?"

"First of all," Luc said. "I want to find out if she truly is being compelled, or having magic used on her. If that's the case, we need to help her get her own free will back. No one deserves to be treated that way."

"Agreed." Uriel nodded and the rest followed suit. "If this is true, I can honestly say, I'm ashamed to call Michael my brother."

"And then?" Gabe asked, finishing off the drink and pouring another. His tolerance was twice that of even Az. Luc would find it impressive, if it wasn't his good whiskey the asshole was drinking.

"And then, I think he will come look for her. It's our best chance of forcing him here, on our terms. You all know damn well that if this were reversed, if I had found my soul mate, Michael would have no problem using her against me."

"True, brother," Az said. "But you're a better man than Michael. You would never hurt an innocent to further your own agenda."

"I wouldn't and I don't intend on hurting Melanie. If she genuinely is in love with Michael, and we succeed in locking him in the Hell Box, I guess she will be quite upset. I would be willing to allow her to see him, or whatever she needs to move on. I'm not trying to be cruel here."

"Why can't we use the mirror on her?" Uriel glanced in the direction of Luc's magic mirror. It was something he hadn't thought of himself and it was brilliant. They could look into Melanie's life, see whatever they could to not only help them decide if she was being compelled, but to gather information on how best they might get to her. That was unless Michael managed to find a way to block them from seeing her.

"Maybe we can." Luc waved his hand in front of the mirror and it came to life, filling with fog, and waiting to show him what he needed. His siblings gathered around him, crowding together.

To make the mirror work, he only needed to think about what he wanted to see, and in this case, it was Melanie. He didn't have much to go on, so the mirror had to work for it. He concentrated on what Cupid told him, then on his brother. The mirror scrolled through women, one after another, trying them on like hats. Just as Luc was about to give up, it stopped. A beautiful, dark haired girl, with sad blue eyes, came into focus.

"Is that her?" Az tried to see past Gabe and Uriel, but just like when they were younger, they pushed him out of the way.

"I have no idea and I'm not about to bring Cupid here to confirm it." Luc willed the mirror to show him the girl in real time. She was sitting alone in a room, on an empty bed, crying. There was no cue as to what upset her, so he flicked his wrist and sent time backward.

The mirror didn't show him Michael, but that didn't surprise him at all. Michael would have made sure no magical devices could pick up on him. But if he thought no one knew about Melanie, then maybe he wouldn't have thought to cloak her as well. It was sloppy on his part, but Luc wasn't going to complain.

Luc went back in intervals, watching the woman's life. She was with her family before she was alone in that room. There was a period of about six months that she was in this new place. Before that, she was happy, around people. After, she was sad, alone. There was an obvious change, and in Luc's mind, the reason was Michael.

"That has to be her." Gabe stepped forward and took a closer look. "This is exactly the type of woman Michael would pick."

Gabe knew him best, so if Gabe believed it was her, then it probably was.

"Okay, so how do we take her?" Az slipped through Gabe and Uriel and touched the glass with two fingers.

"I can handle that part," Uriel said.

They all looked at her, but it was Gabriel that spoke. "How do you plan on doing that?"

"I've learned a few tricks since we were kids." She shrugged. "I can get her to come to me. As long as he's not physically restraining her, I can manage it."

"She's not in shackles right now." Az flicked his hand at the mirror and it went back to real time.

"Then I've got it covered. Do you want her brought here?"

That was a good question. If they brought her there, Michael might be able to get her back. If they brought her to Heaven, he could find her even easier, and they all knew their father wouldn't step in and help. So there was only one option, an option that would require Luc's most trusted demon to sacrifice for.

"I think it's obvious where she needs to go."

"Harley's not gonna like this," Az said, stepping back from the mirror and crossing his arms over his chest. "She wants to be part of this battle. If you send her down there, to babysit no less, she won't be able to participate."

"Yeah, yeah. I know she's gonna be pissed, but what choice do I have? I can't trust anyone else with something so important."

"This is going to move up the time line." Gabe turned to Luc. "You do realize that, don't you?"

"I do. I figure I'll have one more day, if I'm lucky, and then we can finally put an end to this."

This was what Luc had been waiting for. It was what he wanted. Michael threatened everything. But things were going well for him. This month's girl was more than he expected. He wanted to get to know her and figure out if she might be the one he'd been looking for. He didn't want to put things on hold. Hell, he didn't want to spend a single day away from her. But he would have to.

Tomorrow she would be there to shadow him. They would have the day together. For all Luc knew, it could be his last day. Michael could very well kill him. So tomorrow had to count. It had to matter. He took one last look at the sad girl in his mirror. She deserved better too. She needed saving and no one else was going to do it.

∽

Anna showed up dressed like she was going sledding, in the arctic. She had on a puffy coat, hat, gloves, boots, pants with a ridiculous number of buttons, turtleneck sweater, with a hoodie over it, and who knew what else under all that. All this from a woman who danced around the park in only a sweater and pants.

And that day was two degrees colder.

"What's with the north pole gear?" Luc pulled the zipper down on her coat and helped her out of it.

"I don't want to give you any thoughts of what's under all this."

"Oh." Luc laughed. "So to stop me from wanting to make love to you, you decided to layer yourself in everything you had in your closet?"

"Something like that."

"It's not working, just so you know, but you said no sex until you got enough for your story, so I will respect that. Besides, you'll die of heat stroke in here if you keep all of that on."

She looked disappointed, but nodded. "Good."

She followed Luc to his office and took off most of the extra clothes. He wanted so badly to get her out of the rest of it, but if this was possibly their last day together, he wanted to spend it getting to know who she really was. He'd gotten glimpses, but it wasn't enough. She deserved that much. Plus, he'd promised her she would get what she needed for her article. He couldn't leave her hanging with something so important to her.

Luc sat behind his desk and motioned for her to take the seat across from him. It was far more formal than he wanted to be, but the desk served as a barrier, giving him just the bit he needed to keep from throwing her down and ripping off the rest of her clothes.

"So, are there any questions you'd like to ask?"

"Can I record you?"

"I guess so."

She pulled out her phone, opened a recording app, and hit record.

"What did you want to be when you grew up?"

"God." Luc tried to force a laugh, but he was serious. He'd looked up to his father once and wanted to be just like him.

"You have to be serious, Luc. This is important to me."

"I am being serious. That was my first career choice."

"Okay, fine. What about after that?"

"I've tried a lot of things, learned a lot of skills."

"Like what?"

"Like... cooking, and psychology, and I'm technically a lawyer, and—"

"You're what?"

"Yeah, that doesn't usually come up in my mind. I don't know why. My brother Az and I are both attorneys. Neither of us practice, but we are licensed to do so."

She tilted her head and a small smile spread across her lips. "What else?"

"I've done... corrections, you could call it."

"Like for prison?"

"Yeah, something like that. I've also been a soldier and even worked in the medical field for a bit. I guess I had to try out a lot of things to figure out what I wanted."

"And what you wanted was to own a club, a super amazing, fancy-as-fuck club?"

"Are those the exact words you plan on using in the article?"

"I haven't decided." She nibbled at the top of her pen for a moment, then scribbled down something in her notebook. "Maybe."

"What about you? Did you ever want to be anything else?"

She paused the recording and thought for a moment. "I thought about being a photographer. Back home, I had this amazing camera. My dad bought it for me when I graduated high school. No expense spared, all the bells and whistles. I used to take long walks and photograph everything I saw that caught my eye."

"You don't have it anymore?"

"I sold it to move out here. I had to get rid of anything that wasn't going to help me do what I really wanted to do. It hurt to do it, but writing is my passion. Photography was just a hobby."

"And the writing? Journalism is where you want to be? Not the secret love stories?"

"Maybe. I mean, it pays the bills. It allows me to live here. Would I like to write fiction and have it be amazing? Sure. But I'm realistic and I know that the chances of that are slim. So journalism is a good second choice."

Luc frowned. He didn't want her to settle for second choice. He didn't want her to give up a beloved hobby. He wanted her to have everything that made her happy.

She tapped record again and nibbled her pen some more. "How long have you been having shows here?"

"A little over a year. It was Harley's idea to start bringing in entertainment. I had the stage built and the rest is history. Really, I can't take credit for any of it. She does all the work. She finds the acts, books them, and handles just about everything. I don't know what I'd do without her."

"How did you get the money to start this place? It had to be expensive."

"Actually, not as much as you might think. It started as a bar only, which I paid for with the money I had saved from everything I'd done before. Then it grew over time."

"But you had to buy this huge building to begin with. That had to cost a bit."

"It did, but it was in bad shape when I got it and we slowly made it what it is today. Plus, the original owner owed me a favor, so I got a good deal."

"That sounds very mob-ish." Anna laughed. It was a nice laugh and Luc really noticed it for the first time. The way her eyes crinkled up and sparkled only added to the effect.

"Nothing so illicit, I swear. Just an old man, at the end of his life, trying to pay up old debts. Besides, he had no children to leave it to. I'm pretty sure everything I paid him went to a charity."

"Sounds like you have some interesting friends."

"When you skip around through careers trying to find yourself, you meet a lot of interesting people. I don't know that I'd call them friends, because I save that word for something more meaningful, but I have met some unique individuals."

"Can I have some water?"

"Of course. I'm sorry for not asking." Luc reaching into his mini-fridge and grabbed her a fancy bottled water. Then he poured a bourbon for himself.

"Are you an alcoholic?" Her face was straight, serious, but Luc couldn't help but laugh.

"No, Annalee. I'm not an alcoholic. I just enjoy fine things. Does my drinking make you uncomfortable?"

"Not at all. It's just that you seem to do it all day and

night. Though I've never seen you even buzzed. How is that possible?"

"I think if you get to know my family, you'll see we have an unnaturally high tolerance for alcohol. We all drink socially, often, and getting intoxicated is rare." Luc shrugged. "Just lucky, I guess. Tell me about your friends from home."

"My best friend growing up was Patrick. It was platonic on my part, but he always had a thing for me. We were pretty much inseparable from the time we were six. Our mother's were good friends. I'm not sure how I would have survived high school without him."

"Why? Were you bullied?" Luc leaned forward and watched her mouth as she spoke.

"I guess you could call it that. I was the quiet nerdy girl freshman year. Nobody really knew who I was and that was fine. I had Patrick and I was writing a lot of silly poetry. I was happy, ya know?"

"I do." Luc thought about his own childhood, back when things were good and his family was together.

"Then this senior saw me in the hall one night after school. I was at this freshman intro thing we all had to go to, but he was there late, after track or something."

Luc swallowed hard. He hoped her story wasn't about to take a bad turn. He wasn't sure he could handle another of his girls having that narrative.

"He was super hot and popular, and he just bumped into me, like on purpose, as I'm walking down the hall. It was... flirty, but no big deal. I went home and dreamed about having his babies." She laughed.

"As any freshman girl would, I assume." Luc sipped his bourbon.

"The next day in lunch, he jumps into Patrick's seat before he could sit down and put his arm around me. He started asking me questions, wanting to know all about me. I was kind of in shock, but I played along. By the end of lunch, he asked me to hang out. Of course I said yes."

"Of course."

"He met me at the park and we hung out by this huge oak tree, the kind where local kids all carve their names into. He hands me this pocket knife and says, add your name. So I did, and he put his. Then he kissed me. It was a great kiss, my first, but then he started trying to get his hand down my pants and I'm like no way. So I push him off, but he's a jerk about it, and ends up leaving me there alone."

"Teenage boys are dicks."

"Yeah, well this one certainly was. The next day in school, he told the whole school I gave him a blow job in the park. He had a picture of the tree, where we carved our names, to *prove* it. No one believed me, of course."

"Of course."

"So that became my story, the girl who gives out bj's in the park."

"Sounds rough. But you had Patrick?"

"Yeah. He was my person."

"Was?"

"Senior year, there was this rafting trip." Her eyes teared up, but she took a deep breath and pushed them back. "He drowned."

"I'm so sorry. That must have been awful." Luc reached forward and took her hand. She tensed, but didn't pull away.

"It was, but you can't change the past. You can only move forward."

"Or stay stuck. The fact that you didn't, says a lot about you."

"I guess I always felt like I had to do something, ya know, because he didn't get to?"

"I can understand that. I've lost people, never my best friend, but once, I almost lost her. I can only imagine what it's like to actually go through that, because even *almost* is terrible."

"I'm sorry."

"For what?"

"Telling you that whole sad story. You didn't need to know every detail of my life. I'm not even sure why I said all that. Even my roommates don't know any of that."

"Hey," Luc rubbed his thumb over the back of her hand. "I like hearing your stories. I want to get to know you."

She looked up at him with searching eyes, like she was trying to find out why he cared, but didn't want to ask. After a moment, she pulled her hand away and shook off whatever it was she was feeling.

"What's with the giant tattoo?"

Luc was used to that question. It was rare a woman saw him naked and didn't ask about it. "That's my wings."

"Clearly. What made you choose wings though?"

"I didn't really choose them. They chose me. My family, I'm sure you've noticed all the angel names."

"Lucifer, Azrael, Uriel, Gabriel, uh yes. I've noticed."

"Well, it's a family thing, I guess you could say. We all have them."

"All your siblings have giant angel wings on their back?" Her eyes widened.

"We do."

"I guess it would be weird to want to see them all?"

"Um, yes. I don't think Gabriel would be interested in taking his shirt off. Az would happily strip naked for any woman who asked though, so if you're that curious, I'm sure he wouldn't mind."

"You wouldn't?"

"What? Mind?"

"Yeah, I mean, you wouldn't mind if I asked your brother to take off his clothes?"

"I..." Luc paused and smiled. "I wouldn't mind if you asked to see his wings."

Luc would mind very much if Az showed her more than that. He also wished he could show her that his wings weren't really a tattoo, that they were real, that he could fly her anywhere.

"What is this between us?" She was smiling, but Luc knew she wanted a serious answer.

"What do you want it to be?" He wasn't sure of the answer himself yet. He also knew he had to spend the next two months with different women. How was he going to take things where they needed to go with Anna, maybe even fall in love, and then walk away to be with two different women?

"I don't know. I haven't known you a week, but it feels like we have some connection. Is that just the sex? Is it more?" She chugged half her water bottle and gave him a moment to think. He was grateful, but even that reprieve wouldn't give him enough time to come up with an answer.

"I feel that connection, too. The sex is amazing. I mean, I don't need to tell you that. We both know that it is. Although I feel like maybe there's more to it. But I know that with the stuff going on with my family right now, I can't consider what that might be just yet. There's things I need to figure out first."

"Anything you wanna talk about?"

He wanted to talk about it all, spill the whole crazy truth

to her, but he couldn't. She wouldn't believe him if he tried. He'd have to prove to her who he was and he couldn't do that unless she was his soul mate. The rest of the world didn't need to know what he was. He had enough problems as it was.

"Maybe some day."

Anna frowned. "I understand."

"How about we go supervise some deliveries and I show you how orders are done?"

"Sounds great."

"And after that, if you aren't bored to death, I can take you with me to meet with a potential business contact."

"I'd love that."

Luc got up and came around the desk to her. She stood, only inches from him. The electricity was there. The heat was there. Everything in him begged to take her on his desk, to make love to her until she couldn't move. But she needed this story to work. She was depending on this, and with what he was about to face, she might not be able to depend on him to be around to give her more for the article. Today had to count, for her, not for his out-of-control desire for her.

"Okay, let's go."

~

Luc dragged Anna around all day, doing one thing, or another. He answered all her question, both professional, and personal. She learned so much about him and got more than enough to write a great piece on him. She might even have gotten enough to make him a character in her next fiction story.

The way he acted, made her feel like this might be their

last day together. They still had a couple days left in the week, and she didn't want it to be over, but this was supposed to be about the article, not finding a boyfriend. Her career needed to be her focus.

Except every time she caught him looking at her, she knew there could be something more.

At the end of the day, which for Luc was after eight at night, he'd said goodbye to her. They shared one kiss, albeit a fantastic one, then he tucked her into his car, and had Jason drive her home. She didn't want to leave, and he didn't want her to go, but neither said anything about it.

It felt wrong to leave, like if she didn't do anything to stop it, something would change between them. She'd told him things about her life that she hadn't shared with anyone, at least not since Patrick died, and even then, she told Luc more.

She could tell that Luc had a hard time opening up to people, but he'd been open with her. She could tell that he was telling her things he'd never spoken of. He had more to tell, but she thought they'd have more time to get there. Now she wasn't so sure.

It was silly. They'd known each other less than a week. The focus of their relationship, if you could even call it that, was sex. Feelings weren't built on sex. Not even when it was that good. She wasn't even sure she had feelings for him. It was just that every time they made eye contact, she felt like she did.

Georgia and Destiny were watching a movie when she got home. It was almost over and Destiny would be rushing out the door to go to work. Part of her wanted to tell her not to go, to stay with her and talk out everything that was swirling around in her head, but she just squished between them on the couch and watched the last ten minutes of their movie in silence.

After Destiny left, Georgia said she was tired and went to bed. Anna sat alone, in the dark on the couch, for a long time. Her mind was chaos, a jumbled mess of thoughts, and feelings, and regrets. This was the time to write. Maybe not her article yet, but something. She had to release some of the mess in her mind and writing was the best way to do that.

She grabbed her notebook, and her favorite pen, and wrote until her mind was empty.

10

There's no place like home.

Luc walked through the gates of Hell, passing through the invisible security like it wasn't even there. This wasn't the kind of security one could hack. There wasn't a workaround. It was built into the place, designed by dear old dad. The only way to override the way in or out, besides some elaborate blood ritual done only by Luc himself, was by using the Hell Tablet.

And that was permanent.

Even angels in general couldn't gain access to the place. There were exactly two angels who could come and go in Hell with no escort or assistance. And they were Luc and Azrael. Luc for obvious reasons, and Az because he was the delivery boy.

He hated when Luc called him that, but that's why Luc liked it. Basically though, that was his job. Az was in charge of delivering departed souls to their final destination. Whether that was Hell, or back home in Heaven, he shuffled them along to the right place. It used to be a one-man job, but with overpopulation on Earth, he had to take on some help. The help could deliver the souls to the gates, but not actually pass through themselves. So that left only Luc and Az.

There were a few ways into Hell that others could accomplish, but getting out wasn't easy. Actually, it was impossible. Unless they were escorted by Luc or Az. The only exception to that, was Harley. She could leave, but that took a century to accomplish, and a very painful ritual, for both her, and Luc. Like opening his safe, it took the spilling of Luc's blood. And not just any spilling, it had to be willingly.

When Michael had Harley, if he had known the truth, that the safe could be opened if Luc willingly spilled his blood, things may have turned out quite differently. He might have forced Luc into it to save Harley, and Luc might have agreed. If his father had refused to help, Luc wasn't sure what he would have done.

He was glad he never had to find out.

Az had escorted Gabe and Uriel there earlier when they had Melanie. Now they would meet and discuss the final plan, before Michael came looking for his toy. Luc was in Hell every week, to check on things, make sure his management was doing their jobs, and to keep morality high. But he rarely went into the depths where the prisoners were kept. He didn't like it down there. As much as Luc wanted the guilty to be punished, he didn't like seeing it anymore. His siblings would say he'd gone soft, and maybe he had, but he'd seen so much suffering already. He didn't need to see more.

Luc loosened his tie. It was hot, but not like the stereotypical hell fires, pits of lava, and all that burning nonsense.

Hell was more of a barren wasteland, a desert of sorts. They had seasons, to an extent. No snow, or much rain, but it got cold at certain times of the year. Of course in Hell, time worked differently, so you could never be certain when it would be winter, and when it would be summer if you were coming from another realm.

Down in the pits, his siblings set up a table and some chairs around a small circle. Inside the circle was a woman, crouched, covered in dark hair. He couldn't see her face, only the hair that covered as much of her as she could manage. It was like she was hiding under there, because it was all that she had to use as a shield.

The circle was normally where they held someone they wanted to interrogate. Once inside, human souls, or demons, couldn't leave. Luc never tried to put an actual live human in there before, but clearly that worked, too.

It all seemed unnecessary. The poor thing wasn't going anywhere. Where would she go if she tried? She probably didn't even know where she was.

"Lucifer, glad you could join us." Gabriel looked up with a bored expression.

"We just got here, don't listen to him." Az stood up and walked over to Luc. "I brought Oz with us."

Luc looked around. "Where is he?"

"He's with his sister. I didn't think you'd mind and we needed him to assess Melanie for magic. He did some weird juju on her and said that she was definitely under some sort of spell and a strong compulsion."

"And?"

"And he took care of the spell, but we have to wait for the compulsion to wear off, I guess. It's okay I brought him, right?"

Luc nodded. Oz wanted his sister free from Hell. It was his price for helping them. Luc would need to turn her into a demon for that to happen, but she had to agree to it. With Oz here, he could explain all of that and make sure she was on board.

"The circle seems like overkill, don't you think?" Luc looked around at his siblings. "Who's idea was that?"

Uriel and Az looked at Gabriel, and Luc wasn't surprised. Gabe was always on the cold side emotionally. It was probably what he and Michael had most in common.

Luc walked over to the girl, entering the circle with her. He crouched down, and pushed her hair back, then hooked one finger under her chin, and lifted her face up. She'd been crying. Dirt and tears stained her face. Her bottom lip had crusted blood from where she'd been struck.

"Who hit her?" Luc spun around and glared at Uriel and Gabe. It would never have been Az. His brother may be a whore, but he respected women.

Gabe shrugged. "Don't look at me. She was like that when I got here."

"Uriel?"

"I'm guessing it was Michael. I didn't do anything. She practically begged to come with me."

Luc turned back to the frightened woman. She was shaking. "I'm sorry this happened to you, but we have to keep you here for a bit. You'll be safe here. I promise." Luc used his power to make a bottle of water appear and offered it to her. Her eyes widened and she scurried back against the edge of the circle. He put the water down and stepped outside of her circular prison.

"Way to go, Lucifer, scare her more," Gabe said with the same bored look.

"I'm not the one who terrorized her. None of this is my

fault. I'm not even the one who wanted to use her like this. As I recall, Gabe, you were all for it."

"I was wondering if you forgot how to be an angel." Uriel sneered. "You've been acting human far too long. It's good to see you be yourself."

"It was a bottle of water, Uriel." Luc shook his head. "So now we're all here. What are we doing?"

"I was thinking," Gabe said. "That I'd pull her from the compulsion and we'd see how she feels. You are still interested in that, correct?"

"You can do that?" Luc asked, but all eyes were on Gabe.

"I can. I think. Michael and I use similar techniques. We learned most early lessons together."

Luc should have known that those two were so far up each other's asses that they could cancel out each other's compulsion. Luc had been close with Uriel, but he was pretty sure neither of them had that ability.

All archangels could use compulsion, as could some of the simple angels, but they all did it with their own twist. Archangels were especially good at it, so when a human was under it's grasp, it was damn near impossible to overturn. It could wear off if they were in a place like Hell, where the power of other angels was much less effective, but that took time.

And time they didn't have.

Gabriel got up with a dramatic breath, like all of this was such a bother to him, and walked over to the girl. She scratched at the floor, trying to get out of the circle, but with no luck. Gabe crouched down, and grabbed her by the shoulders, forcefully. He wasn't known for gentleness, and Luc knew he'd be rough, but he still hated seeing a woman treated that way.

Luc turned away, not wanting to watch how Gabe handled it.

"This needs to happen," Az said and put a hand on Luc's knee. "I know it's not what you wanted."

"I never wanted any of this. All I wanted was to find a little happiness for myself. Michael is the one who wants to destroy everything. He should be the one paying the price."

"Well isn't he now?" Uriel said, glancing over at the girl. "We have the one he loves, so that has to hurt him."

"Does he though?" Luc asked.

"Does he what?"

"Does he actually love her? Can you imagine Michael actually loving anyone besides himself? I know I can't," Luc said. "It wouldn't surprise me if this was just his attempt at jealousy. It doesn't seem weird to you that as soon as I start looking for a mate, he suddenly turns up with one, that he had to force to care for him?"

"Makes sense to me," Az said. "Michael is a dick."

Gabe looked back at them over his shoulder and glared at Az. He might be helping them, but it was no secret where his loyalties were. He was only helping because he didn't want the humans destroyed. If it were anything different, less catastrophic, Gabe wouldn't be there with them at all. He would be backing Michael one hundred percent.

"I'm not going to pretend I know what Michael's motivations are, and to be honest, I don't care all that much," Uriel said. "I just want to see all of this done with so I can get back to my own life." She glanced around the room with her top lip curled up. "I certainly don't want to be down here."

Uriel wasn't one to be trapped, and in Hell, that's just what she was, since she couldn't go through the gates on her own. Luc was surprised she even agreed to go down there. Not that he wasn't grateful for all her help. Without her, they probably wouldn't have gotten Michael's little slave away from him. So they needed her, and unfortunately, Gabe, too.

After some time, Gabe stood up and went back to his seat. "Let her rest, then she should be fine."

"Now we need to deal with Michael." Uriel pulled her feet up onto the chair and wrapped her arms around her knees. "He won't delay. Real love or not, you took something that belongs to him."

"Technically, you did, but you're right, he will be coming," Luc said.

"Michael will be furious. It will distract him," Gabe said. "This is the time to be ready. When he shows, you have to get him into the box as quickly as possible. No showing off, no rematches, Lucifer. You need to stay focused on the real job here."

"I get that Gabe. I'm not holding grudges. I don't need to prove I can win a fight against Michael. I just want this over."

"Good." Gabe stood up. "Then we go back and wait."

"Az, why don't you take Uriel and Gabe back? I'll get Melanie settled and bring Oz back."

Az nodded and their siblings followed him out. Luc walked back over to Melanie, who was now quietly sobbing on the dirt floor. He extended an arm and helped her to her feet.

"Let's get you somewhere more comfortable." Luc led her to his private quarters and got her settled in his bedroom. There were enough guards around to watch her if it was just a single person to worry about. But he needed to worry about Michael and there was only one demon he trusted.

She would be there any time to take over and he could leave Melanie without worry. Until then, he would stay by her side.

"What is this place?" She asked after returning from the bathroom to get cleaned up.

He debated whether or not to tell her the truth, but he figured that the poor girl had been lied to, tricked, and taken advantage of enough. "This is Hell."

Her eyes widened and her mouth shivered. "Am I dead?"

"No. You're not dead. You're here to keep you away from Michael."

"He said we were in love." She shook her head and sat on the edge of the bed. "Everything feels fuzzy."

"Do you feel like you love him?"

"He frightens me. He talked about crazy things. Apocalypses, and repopulating the world, and all this stuff about us having all these babies. I... I don't know why I said it was okay."

"That wasn't your fault. Michael has powers, he can make you think or feel things, whether you want to or not."

"Is he the devil?"

Luc wanted to laugh, but it wasn't the time for it. "No. Michael is an angel. Technically, I'm the devil, but I'm not going to hurt you."

He would have to take these memories from her before he returned her to her life. That was assuming he won and Michael ended up caged down here in Hell. But for now, he would be honest with her. She deserved that much at least.

Harley knocked and walked in the room.

"This is Harley, a good friend of mine. She's going to stay here and keep you safe."

Melanie nodded and Luc walked into the hallway to speak with Harley before he left.

"I don't like this."

"I know you don't, but I need you here. I can't trust these asshats down here. Who knows if Michael got to anyone.

He's been playing the long game, Harley. This has been in the works for a while. He would have had time to implant spies, or traitors. You're the only one I can trust."

∽

Luc closed the club early, much to the annoyance of the drunken stragglers that hung around hoping for one more dance, or some random person to agree to go home with them. Luc wasn't interested. They could get laid another night. He was more concerned with their safety. The mage might have put protections on the club, but that didn't mean they were safe.

The only thing left to do was to wait. It wouldn't be long. He could feel it in his bones. Michael wouldn't be happy that they'd taken Melanie. Not that he didn't deserve that, and much worse after he took Harley, but Michael never saw his own wrong doings.

Luc climbed the steps to his apartment for what he hoped wasn't the last time. He might be opposed to killing his brother, but he held no illusions that Michael would even think twice about taking Luc's life. Their first battle was different. Their father was there. Even if Michael wanted to kill him then, their father wouldn't have allowed it. This time, they were on their own.

For good measure, he texted Anna and told her he would be busy with family stuff all day tomorrow, just to make sure she didn't show up. Then he had a few guards set up to keep an eye on her. He also had Oz put some protections on her apartment. Luc couldn't guarantee her safety, but he wasn't willing to leave it completely up to chance either.

Before he opened the door to his apartment, he could

hear his siblings arguing. Their constant bickering was getting old. Luc would be a lot happier when they were done with all this nonsense so his siblings could stop being in his space all the time. He'd missed having family in his life, but this was too much.

"Just toss her in with him then," Gabe said, raising his voice. "I don't honestly care, Azrael. What does it even matter?"

"What's going on here?" Luc walked into the apartment, in the middle of his siblings and the room went silent.

"The boys are arguing about what to do with Melanie when all of this is over," Uriel said, with her arms crossed over her chest. She had an amused smile on her lips, enjoying the bickering for some reason. Maybe it reminded her of home.

"Do what you want." Luc left them there and went to his safe. He'd been afraid to open it since he realized that Michael was after the tablet, but he had no choice. Besides, if it was ever a good time since everything started, it was when he had three other angels in the apartment.

Without his siblings realizing what was going on, he opened the wall plate that hide his safe, and grabbed a small knife he left near the bed, to slice across his palm. He pressed his palm into the safe and waited for it to pop open. Beside the Hell Tablet inside the safe, was the Hell Box. Luc snatched it up, shoved it in his pocket, and slammed the safe closed.

"What are you doing in here?" Uriel was standing behind him in the doorway, leaning against it like being in his bedroom was the most natural thing in the world.

"Getting this." Luc pulled the small box out and held it up, then shoved it back in his pocket.

"Is that the Hell Box?" Uriel flashed herself in front of

him, not wasting the extra three seconds it would have taken to walk there. "Can I see it?"

"No."

"Why not?" she whined, the way she did when they were kids. Back then, it often got her what she wanted. Now, he could easily ignore it.

"Because it's not a toy."

"What's not a toy?" Az walked in to see what they were doing.

"He's got the Hell Box in his pocket." Uriel practically bounced in place. It was the most excited he'd seen her since she was young.

"What does he have in his pocket?" Gabe wandered in Luc's bedroom to see what was going on.

"Why is everyone in my bedroom?" Luc pushed past the lot of them and went for his bottle of bourbon. "No one is touching the box. It's staying with me. All of you need to shut the fuck up."

The apartment grew silent.

"I'm going to sleep." Gabe went back into Luc's room and closed the French doors behind him.

"Whatever, I'll be back in a few hours. I need some air." Uriel flashed out of the apartment.

Luc drank down an entire glass of bourbon, which was the last of the bottle, then poured a glass of scotch. It was the only thing his siblings hadn't been sucking down.

"I'll go get you a few more bottles from downstairs." Az headed for the door and for the first time since he walked in, Luc felt like he could take a breath.

He loosened his tie and slipped it off his head, then took off his jacket and tossed it on the chair. He wasn't in the mood to sleep on his couch. He wanted his bed back, and his bedroom, and his entire apartment. And maybe his life.

Luc just needed to decompress. He headed for the couch, with the bottle of scotch, since apparently Az was taking forever to return with the good stuff, when he saw the usual angel flash come from the kitchen. It was too fast for Uriel to be back and he was pretty sure he had Az better trained to use the door, but maybe not.

"Az, I thought we talked about you—"

Luc stopped in his tracks.

It wasn't Az.

"Surprise, brother." Michael took a few steps closer, then stopped.

"Michael," Luc said, feeling for the box, and realizing it was in his jacket pocket, that he just flung over the chair. "Showing up uninvited I see. You never did have manners."

"Maybe not, Lucifer, but I've always had everything else you wanted."

"I'm not sure where you've gotten that idea from, but you have nothing I want."

"Well this time, you have something I want."

"So I've heard. Actually, I have several things you might want, starting with your lackey."

"Where is our little Cupid, anyway?"

"Locked up, like *you're* going to be."

Michael laughed. It was loud enough for Gabriel to hear, even if he'd fallen asleep, but for some reason, he wasn't coming. If that asshole had changed his mind about being on Luc's side, he was going to lock him in the box with Michael when all this was over.

"You should want this too, Lucifer. I'll empty Hell and you won't have to be stuck there anymore. You can even go back home and make nice with Daddy. I'll take it all from here."

"You could have had it, Michael. You're the one who

chose to take it upon yourself to have me banished to Hell. Father would have put you in charge. It would have been yours."

"It still will be, as well as this filthy planet. But I'll remake it, much better than how the humans have it. They destroy. I'll perfect."

"With your little slave? You can't even get a woman to fall in love with you on your own, so you have to compel it? That's pathetic."

Michael balled his fists at his sides and took a couple more steps toward Luc. His jacket was too far to reach. He needed to get closer without Michael realizing what he was doing. And where the fuck was Gabriel? Luc glanced at his bedroom door and Michael smiled.

"Are you waiting for Gabe to help you?" Michael took another step. "Don't hold your breath. I sensed him the second I got within ten miles of this place. The first thing I did was take care of him."

Luc took a step backwards, toward the chair. He wasn't sure he wanted to know exactly what Michael was talking about, but he knew he couldn't count on Gabe coming to help now.

"And Azrael, well, not only is he not coming, but well, I'm sorry. I know he was your favorite."

Luc couldn't think about what might have happened to Az. If he survived this, he could worry about it then. For now, he had to keep his focus. He needed to get to the box and he needed to get Michael into it.

"Well, I guess we're even then for Melanie."

Michael pressed his lips together and held his breath. He was trying to keep his cool, but Luc saw through it. He was pissed, which actually amused Luc more than it should in this situation.

"Humans are expendable. I can find five others just like her."

"And then force them to fake-love you? Aww poor Michael. You must be really bad in bed if even as an angel, you can't get a chick to fall for you."

Michael pulled a bright, silver dagger from his jacket and held it at his side. Luc recognized the blade. It was one forged a long time ago that their father kept in a glass box back home and called the forever blade. As children they all learned the story about the blade that could kill an angel, for good. Luc always thought it was screwed up that such a thing existed, not to mention that they were basically threatened with it as small children.

So, Michael really did wish him dead.

Luc used his powers to call his own blade. It wasn't one that would kill his brother. He wouldn't have used one if he did have it, which he didn't. But he needed to defend himself, one way or another. If he could hold Michael off, maybe even long enough for Uriel to return, if she even could, then maybe he had a chance. What he really needed was that box.

Luc took a few more steps in the direction of his jacket and Michael took a few more toward him.

"Are you planning on finishing off all of our siblings, brother?"

"Only the ones who get in my way. If you'd like to hand over the tablet and walk away, I would consider letting you go, Lucifer."

He was lying, but even if he wasn't, Luc would never give him that tablet. If Michael killed him, the safe would never open. Not unless their father decided to intervene, which he never would. Michael didn't know that, of course, and Luc wasn't about to tell him. He refused to give him any clue to how the safe worked.

Maybe with enough time and magic, he would find a way in. There were no guarantees where Michael was concerned. Luc wouldn't put it past him to one day find a way in. But his safe was built by their father and it was made that way for a reason. It required not only Luc's blood, but for it to be given willingly. That wasn't possible with him dead.

"You'll never get that tablet, Michael. You're just too stupid to realize it. It's a shame that dad made you the way he did. I think even Cupid made out better than you did. At least he's intelligent. Oh, and good looking."

Michael tensed and advanced a few more steps.

He was always self-conscious of his looks. As an angel, he was perfect, of course, but Michael's beauty was more subtle than many of their siblings, and he always felt inferior because of it. It didn't matter that compared to humans, Michael would be a supermodel. He never saw that when he looked in the mirror. Luc hoped he never would.

"Not only will I get the tablet, but I'll use it, destroy everything you've built here, and maybe I'll even replace Melanie with one of your little game girls."

"My goodness did she scream. Melanie doesn't take to pain well. Did you know that?" The lies didn't even bother Luc. Being honest wouldn't piss off Michael, and right then, it was all he had. "You probably did, since you had no problem roughing her up."

Michael practically growled and lunged for Luc. Luc just managed to get out of the way. Lucky for him, he ended up closer to the jacket. Not close enough, but closer was better than further away.

"I wonder if she screamed as much as your little demon

pet when I sliced her open." Michael's eyes twinkled while he likely recalled the memory. "Has she told you all the fun things we did together?"

"Fun? She said it was the most boring week of her life. You might need to step up your game. By the way, did I mention that it was Harley that was with Melanie at the end?" Luc felt the need to throw in at least a bit of the truth there.

"I'm really going to enjoy stabbing this thing into your heart, Lucifer. I've waited a long time for this."

"That's really sad, Mike. You might want to take up a hobby and stop being so obsessed with me. It's pathetic."

Michael lunged again and sliced Luc's arm. It was deep enough to hit bone, but Luc merely winced. He wouldn't let Michael have the satisfaction of knowing he'd hurt him. Blood ran down his arm and dripped onto his carpet. It was going to be a bitch to clean that up.

Luc was in this alone. Who knew what Michael did to Gabe and Az. He didn't even know if Uriel was all right, or if she was, if she would make it back. With the sigils Oz set up, she should have been warned when Michael showed up. The fact that she wasn't there, gave Luc a sick feeling in the pit of his stomach.

Once again, Michael went at Luc. This time, he didn't try to duck, but instead lunged back, jabbing the dagger into Michael's chest. He yelled in pain and Luc pulled the blade out, then jumped back. Michael gripped the wound and his eyes went red. There was little recognizable in them. It was as if the brother he'd grown up with, the one he'd once looked up to, then hated for so long, wasn't even in there. He was gone.

In a fury, Michael came at Luc again, this time with only murder on his mind. He was going to kill Luc. This was his only chance. Michael leaped onto Luc, knocking them both, and the chair to the floor. Michael stabbed the blade at Luc, over and over, making contact with his chest, arms, and even slicing his face, over and over, he continued his frenzied assault.

Luc did his best to fight back, to at least injure Michael enough to buy himself some time to get to the box. His jacket was so close. If he could just reach it, before Michael could make contact with his heart.

Millimeters from Luc's heart, Michael jabbed the dagger into Luc's chest again, piercing his lung. The metal bit into him like molten lava. The burning sucked any oxygen he had out. He reached with one hand for the jacket, and held Michael back with the other. But he was growing weaker. Again, Michael was going to win. Luc wasn't strong enough.

Michael raised the dagger over his head and smiled. "I've waited so long for this. I'm almost sorry it's about to be over. I have to know one thing though."

Luc just stared at him, not sure if he could even talk at that point.

"Why didn't you bring something that could kill me? You have to know that stupid blade you called up can only wound me. You've had all this time to prepare, and yet, you weren't even close to ready for this battle."

Maybe it wasn't his best choice, but Luc stood by his decision not to kill his brother. Even though Michael had no such reservations, and Luc was about to die, he would let that task be on Michael's head, not his own. He would go to his eternal sleep with a clear conscience.

Michael shrugged. "Oh well. I guess it doesn't matter."

Luc closed his eyes, readied for death, when a flash of light burned his lids, and he heard his name yelled out.

Both Luc and Michael turned at the same time, just as Uriel placed the box into Luc's hand.

"You can't be—" Michael started to say just as Luc pressed the box into his bleeding chest to activate it with Luc's blood. It erupted into blinding light, too powerful for Luc to even hold onto for long. With his last shred of strength, he thrust it at Michael, before the whole world went black.

11

The bright sunlight that shone through the window was too harsh. Luc squeezed his eyes shut and groaned. He wasn't sure where he was, because it certainly wasn't his own bed. He would never have allowed that kind of light to be in his face in the morning. He tried to move, but everything hurt. It felt like he'd been hit by a truck. Then backed over by it, then thrown off a cliff, after being set on fire. Also, doused in salt, covered by stones after hitting the bottom, and finally run through a cheese grater.

Basically, he was in agony.

He was pretty sure he was alive, because death couldn't be that painful. Not the kind of death an angel had when killed with the forever blade. The fact that he was still able to think, clued him in on the fact that he wasn't dead, but it took him a few minutes to process it. Bits and pieces came back in waves. He remembered Michael showing up and he remembered the fight. He was alone, and Michael was winning, again.

But then he wasn't alone.

Uriel was there.

And so was his father.

Luc used every ounce of strength he had left and pushed himself up on his arms to look at the grave faces frowning down at him.

"What's going on?" His voice came out in a croak, the dryness of his throat preventing anything further. Uriel handed him a glass of water and helped him drink down half of it. Then she sat on the edge of the bed and frowned. He had to look as bad as he felt.

"How do you feel?" his father asked him, with that same grave frown that Uriel had.

"Like I died."

"You did." His father turned his head away. "I brought you back."

The words echoed in Luc's head at a deafening level.

"Why?" It was all he could think and the word just fell out of his mouth.

His father snapped his head around to stare at him. Luc couldn't tell if he was angry, or hurt. Maybe it was both.

"You're my son and I love you."

Luc wanted to say something snarky, or sarcastic, but he didn't have it in him. He was glad to be alive, even if it hurt this much. Even if he owed his life to his father.

"Father says your injuries will heal soon. It took a lot to bring you back." Uriel tried to force a smile, but it wasn't believable.

"Michael?" Luc grabbed Uriel's hand. He didn't care what happened to him if Michael succeeded and found a way to get the tablet.

"He's in the box. You don't remember?"

He didn't. Not really. He remembered Uriel thrusting the box into his hand, then he remembered a blinding light. He thought that was his death and maybe it was. But maybe it was Michael being sucked into the box. Maybe it was both things simultaneously. None of it mattered. He was currently alive and Michael was trapped in the box where he couldn't hurt anyone.

Luc closed his eyes. He could finally have peace.

"Where are Gabe and Az?" He opened his eyes again and Uriel burst into tears, then ran from the room.

That couldn't be good.

Luc looked at his father who was staring out the window in silence.

"Dad?" Luc propped himself higher and swung his legs over the side of the bed. He attempted to stand and fell flat on his face. Immediately, he tasted the coppery tang of blood in his mouth, and he swiped at his bottom lip with the back of his hand.

"What are you doing?" His father was to him in an instant, lifting him off the floor, and returning him to the bed. "You need to rest. It was a lot of work to bring you back. I don't have the strength to do it a second time." He handed Luc a wad of tissues to stop the flow of blood from his mouth.

"Tell me where Gabe and Az are."

His father sat on the edge of the bed and looked down. He took a deep breath, then met Luc's eyes. "Michael killed them both before he got to you. He stabbed the forever blade through their hearts. Gabriel never saw it coming. Azrael put up a fight."

The words were making no sense. Luc had been killed by the same blade. He was here, so why weren't his brothers. This was *God* they were talking about. If he brought Luc back, why not his brothers?

"Bring them back." Luc tried to fight off the blanket his father had tucked over him. "And let me up."

"So you can fall on the floor again? You're too weak, Lucifer. You need to stay in bed." His father sighed, a deep, soul crushing sigh. "I'm trying to bring Gabriel back. It takes a lot of energy to bring back an archangel, son. It was nearly all I had to bring you back. That dagger was called the forever blade for a reason."

"So bring Az back. He's only a baby archangel, hardly a real one at all. It should be easier." Luc struggled, but his father held him there.

"It won't be easier. Azrael might be much younger, and seem less than your original siblings, but he isn't. My power isn't unlimited, as much as you might think it is."

"I don't care. Let Gabe stay dead then. I need Az back." Tears welled in Luc's eyes. "You owe me this much. All of this is your fault."

And it was. The animosity between Michael and Luc, the fact that Luc had the tablet to begin with, and their father's refusal to stop things from getting to where they did, all of it, was his fault.

"I haven't asked you for much, ever, and even when I have, you've always had strings attached, strings that make coming to you usually not worth it. But this time, I need you to help. I need you to bring Azrael back."

"I can't, son."

"You created an entire universe. You were able to make angels, humans, animals, and everything in between. Why the hell can you not bring one more angel back?"

"Because that blade was meant to be a forever death. I designed it that way, not to be bypassed. In order to bring you back, I lost something permanently, something that will likely prevent me from making more creations in the future."

"Fuck creating things. Just bring Az back!"

"Lucifer, if I could do it, I would. I'm not even sure if I can get Gabe back."

"You shouldn't have saved me then. You should have brought Az back first." Luc struggled, tried to fight his father off, but it was no use. The old man was right. He was too weak.

His father put his hand on the side of Luc's face. There were tears in the older man's eyes as well. Then he shook his head, touched Luc's forehead, and everything went dark.

~

"I CAN'T BELIEVE you insisted on coming back here already, or at all." Uriel scrunched her nose up and looked around the apartment. The place was trashed. Broken furniture, burn marks on the walls, blood stains. His bed was gone completely. The reminder that Gabriel had died in it was no less by it not being there. At least the couch was somewhat intact, but of course, his favorite chair was in a splintered mess on the floor.

Uriel raised her hand to, what Luc assumed, was to use her powers to fix the place, but Luc stopped her.

"Don't."

"Why the hell not? This place is a disaster."

"It is and it will be cleaned, but not like that." Luc hobbled over to the couch and slumped into it.

Even he wasn't sure why he'd returned. His father offered for him to stay a while. He hadn't said permanently, though. He still expected Luc to stay in charge of Hell, and of his murderous brother who would forever reside there in the box. It was a big ask and he knew it. At the very least, the old man could have taken control of the box and kept

Michael with him. Who knew, maybe one day he could be rehabilitated.

While Az would still be dead.

"Is Harley back?"

"She is. I helped erase the memories from the girl Michael had and we sent her home. I don't think she will ever be the same though. He damaged her for good." Uriel sat down next to Luc. "Is there anything you need?"

"Are you leaving?"

"For a bit yes. I'll be back, though. You can't get rid of me anymore."

She felt bad for him. The pity was clear in her eyes, but Luc couldn't stand to lose another person he cared about, so he would take it. She was the only blood family he had left in his life.

"Any chance there's any bourbon in here?" Luc glanced over at the bar, then realized that's where Az was going when Gabe killed him.

Uriel snapped her fingers and handed him a bottle. If only he hadn't insisted Az act human, then he would have done the same, rather than going down to the bar alone, and he might still be alive. Luc took the bottle, but set it down next to him. He wasn't in the mood for a drink anymore.

"Lucifer," Uriel said and stood up. "Azrael left you a letter. I found it in his pocket when I brought his body back home." She pulled a folded envelope from her pocket and held it out. Luc stared at it for a long moment, unable to touch it. "Okay, well I'll just leave it for you." She placed it on the couch next to him and flashed out of the apartment.

Luc got up and walked to the window. His whole body still hurt, but he welcomed the pain. At least with pain, he knew he was still alive. Besides, he deserved what he got. He was alive and Az was dead. It was his fault. If he'd never let him hang around, never let him be part of this fight, never made him stop using his powers when he was on Earth, he would be fine. He'd be off on some island somewhere, sipping whiskey, and having orgies.

Now he was dead.

Luc glanced back at the letter.

And the bottle of bourbon.

He chose the bourbon.

After making it back to the couch and twisting off the top on the bottle, he drank half of it down. Then he sat there, with the bottle between his thighs, feeling sorry for himself. After a while, he drank the other half, finally feeling a glimpse of intoxication, before Harley walked in and sat down next to him. She picked up the letter and put it on his leg.

"You should read that."

"Why?"

"Because those are his last words to you. He wanted you to read it."

"Did you read it?"

"Of course I did. I'm a god damned demon. You think privacy means shit to me?"

Luc wasn't surprised, or angry. It actually made him feel better to know Harley read it and still thinks he should. She knew him better than anyone, so if she thought he could handle it, then he could.

"Want me to get some guys up here to start cleaning up?" Harley kicked a piece of the old coffee table and glanced around the room.

"I might do it myself."

"Have you looked in a mirror? I think the most you

should be moving around is to open the door when the guy comes with your new bed today."

"New bed?"

"I assumed you didn't want to sleep on this broken couch, so I ordered you a new one. The new couch will be here tomorrow, with a coffee table. I found nearly an identical couch, but the old coffee table wass shit, so I picked out something different. You have lousy taste."

Luc didn't care what table she picked out. It didn't matter much anyway. "Thanks."

There was a part of him that wanted to move somewhere else. The idea of living in the place where two of his siblings died, at the hand of his own brother, seemed wrong. But he loved this place. He couldn't let Michael take that from him, too.

"Is the bar open?"

"I reopened it yesterday. I figured you'd want me to."

Luc wasn't even sure how long it had been. A few days? A week? Maybe two? He'd spend the first who knew how many days mostly sleeping back in Heaven. The whole thing was starting to blur. If that was his own mind, or something his father planted the seed for, he wasn't sure, but he was grateful. No one needed vivid details of such horrors.

"Have you spoken with Anna?" Luc had been dreaming about her while he was away, but he hadn't asked anyone about her. Did she know something was wrong? Had anyone bothered to tell her anything, or did she think he was avoiding her?

"I have. She came by while the place was still closed. She's been worried about you."

"But she's okay?" He figured that if Michael had gotten to her, someone would have mentioned it already, but he couldn't be one hundred percent sure until it was confirmed.

"She's fine. She handed in her article. It made the cover, but they had to use some older photos of you since you couldn't do new ones. She did a great job." Harley pulled out her phone, clicked a few things, then held it out so he could see.

"I'll read it later." Luc shook his head and ran his finger over the letter sitting on his thigh.

"Okay, well I'll leave you in your squalor then. I gotta get back down there. I'm training a new bartender and he's a complete moron."

"Why did you hire him then?"

"He looks pretty and I like tips." She shrugged and headed out the door.

Luc stared at the letter for a long time. It felt warm on his leg, like the paper itself was willing him to touch it. He wasn't ready. He probably never would be. But he picked it up, pulled the letter from the envelope, and unfolded the paper. Luc could make out Az's scent on it and it was almost enough to make him shove it back in the envelope. Instead, he took a deep breath, and read.

To my favorite brother,

Read in scary ghost voice If you're reading this I'm dead...

Okay, fine, just read it in a normal voice, because let's face it, I'm probably not around to be a ghost. I know I was always the goofy little brother, who hung around like a pest, but admit it, I've grown on you. I know you're probably wishing I hadn't, because then saying goodbye to me would be easier. But I want you to know something, I would have given my life ten times over to have the time we had together.

I wrote this letter because let's face it, me surviving a battle with Michael is slim, but don't think that for one second, I regret it. I don't. Although, I do hope we won, because if not, then you're dead too, and no one is reading my letter. Okay, no, Harley is probably standing there with her nose in it, but that's okay, because she should know that I loved her too. She was always like the older sister who likes to bully her siblings. I loved that about her.

Assuming we won, and you survived though, I want to tell you a few things. You have to finish the game. I know right here is where you think about putting the letter down and cursing me out loud. Go ahead, I'll wait. Okay, are you done? Good. Now, you have to finish the game and find your true love. It's the only way I'll be at peace. You need to know that you deserve this, Lucifer. You deserve true love more than anyone I've ever known. Also, I already know which sin you're going to pick. Ask Harley when it's over and she can tell you. I wouldn't be able to stand it if you gave up because of me.

One last thing, maybe don't tell Sarah I'm dead. Let her think I'm a dick who ran away. I'd rather she hated me, than grieved me. She deserves better, too. Now get your pathetic, crying ass up, and live your life. I am assuming you've shed a few tears, because if not, damn, you're a shit brother. Just kidding. I love you.

. . .

Az.

Luc swiped the tears from his face and put the letter back in the envelope. It was all he could do to breathe. After a few minutes, he stuffed the envelope into his pocket, and stood. His whole body hurt, but that was okay. He was going to clean his apartment and wait for his new bed to arrive. He would honor Az. He would move forward. He had no idea how that was going to happen yet, but he would do his best to try.

For Az.

~

Once the apartment was looking better, and the delivery guys showed up to drop off the new bed, Luc made his way downstairs to the club. Everything looked the same, but it all felt completely different. He wasn't sure if there was any mess from that night, but since his father had said that Az put up a fight, he imagined there had been. Harley would have cleaned that up first. There was no way she would have let him see any evidence of his little brother's death.

Luc glanced around, through the people dancing and having a good time, and wondered where Az had died. It could have been anywhere from the stockroom, to the bar area, to anything in between. He thought he would feel it, like he would just know where it happened, but he didn't. He could ask, but then he wasn't sure he really wanted to know.

"Shouldn't you be in bed?" Harley asked as Luc slipped

onto a barstool and helped himself to a glass. She slapped his hand before he could grab the bourbon bottle and poured him a double.

"It just came. I cleaned up." Luc gulped down half the bourbon and put the glass down. "Maybe I should go see Anna?"

"Maybe you should wait until your face heals up. I told her there was a break in and you got hurt, but that you'd be okay. If she sees you like this," Harley waved a hand in front of Luc's face. "She's gonna know you were dead."

"I thought it would heal faster."

"To be honest, so did I. But apparently, when you get murdered with a dagger meant to destroy angels for good, this is the best you can do."

"I don't get it." Luc shook his head. "We were all taught, like had it drilled into our heads, that if we were to die from that blade, we were done with for good. No take backs, no passing go, no soul moving on. I know he's God, but he designed this blade to be forever."

"Uriel talked to me about it a little. She said that what he left out was that your soul, should you be killed with it, is returned to him. It's not in its right form, but it's there. He used that, and I guess a whole lot of almighty creator juju, to bring you back. He's still trying to get Gabe back."

Harley was quiet for a moment, then she continued. "She also told me that the thing he had to do to get you back, it was like cutting off both his arms and legs, and losing a kidney. He had to give something major up to get it to work. There's just not enough to keep doing that."

It was just like him to leave that part out. Luc was surprised his father chose to bring him back over Gabe, not knowing if it would even be possible to get them both returned to the living. Never in a million years, would he think he'd be first choice.

He wished he wasn't. He would rather have Az brought back first. Luc would gladly give up his life to save his brother. Their father had to have known that.

"I know he wants me to continue with the game."

"Oh." Harley shrugged. "I figured you'd wait like a week to read that letter. You do tend to brood."

"I don't brood. And no, I read it a few hours ago."

"So you want me to start thinking about the next sin?"

"No, that's why I'm bringing it up. He wants me to continue, and for him, I will, but I need some time."

"I'll give you a few weeks. Technically, your month with Anna isn't up completely, so you'll have that, but I'm not waiting too much longer. You have to get back on the horse, Lucifer."

"I'm not riding a horse Harley. My brother died. I died. Give me a second to process that."

Harley nodded and topped off his drink. She left him alone with his thoughts and stuck the bottle of bourbon next to him on the bar. He would need at least that much. Not that it would change anything. It couldn't bring Az back, or stop anything Michael did. It couldn't give his father whatever it was he needed to perform a couple more miracles. All it could do was numb some small bit of his pain and help him get through the day.

At least he had Anna to look forward to. She was the one bright spot in this whole miserable year. As soon as he healed a bit more, he would get to see her and maybe things would feel more normal again. Nothing would ever be the same, but maybe with her, they could be okay.

12

It had been three weeks since he'd been home. Three weeks that he kept telling himself he was going to call Anna, that he didn't. Now she was standing at his door with a suitcase and a package wrapped in pretty colored paper. Her eyes were sad, but it wasn't about him.

"Come in." He stepped aside and invited her into his apartment, for the first time. Everything was cleaned up, fixed, or replaced. It looked like nothing bad had ever happened there.

"Nice place." She glanced around, still clutching her suitcase handle and the gift.

"Thank you. Can I take your coat?" It was the first time he'd seen her appropriately dressed for the weather.

She put the suitcase down on the floor, handed him the package, and slipped out of her coat. He handed her the gift back and took her coat, then hung it on the rack behind the door.

"This is for you." She thrust the gift back into his hands. "I didn't want you to have it like this, but I have to leave, so this is all I can do."

"Leave?" Luc shook his head. "What do you mean?" He looked down at the suitcase and his stomach dropped.

"I'm going home." Her words hung in the air like a thick blanket. Luc wanted her to take them back, to say she was joking, but he knew by her face that it wouldn't happen.

"Why?" He took a step toward her and stopped. "Your article made the cover. It was fantastic. I read it."

"It's not that. The story went great. I even got a promotion." She kept her head down and picked at her thumbnail.

"So why are you leaving?"

"My father had a stroke. I have to go home and take care of him. It's too much for my mother alone."

Luc wanted to offer her money for a caregiver, or to heal the man with his powers, or anything that would keep her in his life, but he couldn't. All he could do was watch her walk out of it.

So he nodded. "I'm so sorry to hear that. Is there anything I can do?"

"You can read that." She motioned to the package in his hands. "It's my first complete romance novel."

Luc looked down at the gift in his hands and smiled for the first time since that night. "Congratulations."

"I wanted to thank you."

"What for?"

"For encouraging me, for motivating me, and well," she looked down and blushed. "For being my muse."

Luc's smile widened. "Glad I could help."

Anna leaned in, popped up on her toes, and kissed him. It wasn't the raw, ravenous kisses they normally shared. This one was soft, sweet, and it was a clear goodbye.

She grabbed her coat from the rack, pulled it back on, and started to leave. Before she could get through the door, he grabbed her arm to stop her.

"I don't want you to go." He tossed the novel on the table near the door and held her face in his hands.

"I'm sorry." A small tear escaped her eye and Luc wiped it away with his thumb. "I don't want to go."

Luc searched her eyes for one last second, then kissed her the way she deserved to be kissed. It wasn't the simple, sweet goodbye that she'd just given him. It was desperate, emotional, and it released everything he'd been feeling the past few weeks. By the time she pulled away, she was full on crying.

Without another word, she spun around and left.

~

THERE WERE NO MORE BREAK-INS. Sarah Ward and her partner caught a few of the guys involved, and had them locked up in jail. Slowly, everything returned to normal around the club. People kept showing up, getting drunk, and keeping the place going. Luc was grateful that Harley hadn't pushed him on getting on with the next sin, but he knew it had to happen. Nothing was going to take away the pain of losing Az, but he needed to honor him by not wasting his life.

"I think the next sin should be pride," Luc said coming into his office where Harley was doing paperwork.

"Huh?" She had the glasses that she never needed, slipped down her nose, and it made Luc smile. He was learning to enjoy the little things, the way his brother always had.

"I'm ready." He wasn't, but it was as close as he was going to get.

Harley stared at him for a few moments, then hopped up. "Okay. I'll get right on that. You can finish this crap up."

"Hey." He caught her arm before she could get past him. "If you need to talk about anything, you can, ya know?"

"Me? You're the girl in this relationship, Lucifer. I'm fine." She shrugged him off. "Did you finish your love story?"

"If you mean Anna's book, then yes. It was really good. I can't say it's the kind of thing I'm used to reading, but she's talented. I'm really proud of her for finishing it, and for letting it go."

"Maybe I should give it a read?"

Luc laughed. "Now that would be funny."

"Oh?" She raised one eyebrow. "Funnier than the King of Hell reading a romance novel?"

Okay, maybe she had a point.

"I know a guy in publishing. I was thinking about passing it along."

"Maybe you should ask her first?"

"Maybe," Luc said. "But I'm not sure it's the right time to call her. I'm sure she's got enough on her mind."

Harley shrugged and disappeared from the room.

Luc finished up the paperwork and headed back upstairs. His plan was to go to bed. It was late, and he was exhausted, but as he walked past the mirror, he got off track. Without giving it much thought, he waved his hand over the glass and let his mind wander. The first place it went was to Anna.

It was earlier in the day and she was at her father's bedside. He didn't look too bad. He was having some trouble feeding himself, but he was talking pretty well. There were some stumbles here and there, but overall, for a guy who had a massive stroke, he was doing well.

The guy had cut Anna out of his life for wanting to follow her dreams, but when he needed her, she went running back. That was family though. When you had people who cared about you like that, it didn't matter what hurts there were in the past, they came running back to stand by your side.

At least the ones that mattered did.

Uriel had been there for Luc, when he'd needed it most. If not for her, Michael wouldn't have been trapped in the box. His father still would have brought him back, but for what? To what? Uriel was the reason for his second chance.

She'd been gone since he'd been back, but she texted him every day to check in. It was good to have her back in his life. If she'd been gone for good, too, he wasn't sure he could handle it. Michael had taken enough from him.

Luc waved his hand in front of the mirror, and again, let his mind wander. This time the fog cleared and it showed him Talia. She was sitting on the floor in a group, playing a video game. They were arguing over who should go down the left lane, and he was pretty sure, she was winning. She looked happy, like things were finally turning around for her. He was happy for the small part he'd played in that. She wasn't his soul mate, but she was his friend, and he needed all the friends he could get these days. Soon, he would have to call her, make a time to hang out. He was just about ready for another sappy movie and her head on his shoulder.

Once more, he waved his hand, and the fog took Talia away. It settled down, revealing Ronnie. She was sitting on her front porch, looking up at the stars. More than anything, that didn't include do overs and bringing dead brothers back to life, Luc wished he was there with her. Ronnie was his first sin girl, and she would always be special for it, but it was more than that. She calmed him, brought him a peace within his mind that no one else ever had.

Without thinking it through, Luc found himself

standing in front of her. She looked down to see him, not realizing that he wasn't there a second before, and smiled.

"Hi."

He didn't respond. Instead, he walked up the stairs and sat next to her. She snuggled against him, nuzzling her face into his side. She was freezing, so he wrapped his arm around her and pulled her closer into him. Her warmth spread across him, bringing a little life back into him. It was like he'd been frozen all this time and she was the one to melt through it.

They stayed there for a long time, past the time when her teeth started to chatter, and she shivered nonstop against him. Eventually, she started to doze in his arms, and he carried her inside, up the stairs, and put her into bed. She wriggled out of her coat and boots and started taking off the clothes underneath. Luc stopped her, kicked off his own shoes, and climbed in, fully dressed, next to her.

She didn't complain, or protest. Instead, she let him wrap her into his body, and molded around him. He listened to the sound of her heartbeat long after she fell asleep. It was like the ticking of an old grandfather clock. Tick-tock, tick-tock, it lulled him, brought him closer to the peace he felt when he was with her.

Being there with her, hell even looking in on her, was cheating according to Harley. Luc knew she wasn't going to give him shit over it right now, and honestly, he didn't care either way. Tonight, Luc needed this. He needed to be one place where he felt normal, where the rest of the world didn't matter, and where he didn't have to see anyone look at him with pity, or want something from him.

Tomorrow, he would suck it up and keep going. He would let Harley pick a new girl and he would get to know her. He would stop looking in on Anna and face the fact that she was gone, out of his life, even if he might have thought there was a real chance she was the one.

But tonight, he would lay in Ronnie's bed, hold her as tight as he could, and let the world screw off. Tonight, he would do what he needed to do to take care of himself. Az had told him to go see Ronnie, before he met Annalee. Maybe he should have listened. It might have made it easier, given him some distance in his heart from Anna, made it easier to watch her walk away.

Unfortunately, he couldn't go back. If he could, there were a lot of things he would change. None of them would be meeting Ronnie. She would always be his favorite part of this game, even if she wasn't his soul mate, even if he eventually found her, Ronnie would always remain special.

∽

"LOOKS LIKE YOU FINALLY SLEPT." Harley handed Luc a bourbon, and went about cutting limes for the evening rush that was hours away. "The bags under your eyes were starting to irritate me."

"Glad I could save you from that annoyance." He left out the part that it was with Ronnie Falcon that he'd gotten that sleep with.

"Your face looks better too. I think that one might scar, but not as bad as I thought it would."

"I don't scar." Luc scoffed.

"No? Well, then good. I didn't want to say, but it definitely makes your face less pretty. Though it probably ups your street cred quite a bit."

"I'm already the King of Hell, how much more street cred do I need?" Luc gulped down half his drink and stared at her.

"You're right. You got this shit in the bag."

"How's it coming with the next sin?"

"Pride is a hard one." Harley shrugged and put the knife down. "I've got a few options, but I'm not really feeling it. I might need a few more days."

"I'm sure you'll pick someone great." He wasn't, and honestly, he didn't care all that much. Luc was just trying to get through the last two girls and get the game over with. He still wanted to find his soul mate, but the game felt tainted. He was only agreeing to finish it out because it was Az's dying wish. It was just like the little twit to force him into this.

"Of course I will. All the girls I picked were great."

"I can't argue there. Each one had great qualities, and I'm a better person for knowing them, but to be honest, you gave me more hurdles than seems fair."

"What does that mean?" Harley popped out her hip and rested her hand on it. "Any one of those girls could have been a great match for you."

"That's true, in a perfect world. But this isn't a perfect world. Things don't always work out how we want. Sometimes it doesn't matter how much we care about something, or how much we want it to work, it just doesn't." Luc let out a long breath. "I'm not saying that's your fault. It is what it is. Life is just unfair."

And it was.

Luc never bothered to convince himself that anything different was true. He'd learned from a young age that the universe conspired against good, that evil often won out, and that no matter what you did, things wouldn't always work out. It was the way of life. Whether it was here on Earth, down in Hell, or even up in Heaven, that's how it was.

Harley's eyes widened, as she looked at something behind Luc. He spun around to see what she was looking at.

"Hello, brother." Gabriel stood several feet behind Luc, with a somber expression on his face. After Luc's initial shock wore off, he walked over and pulled Luc into an unexpected hug. "I'm really sorry about Azrael. I know you two had a special bond."

Luc didn't want to hear Az's name come out of Gabe's mouth. He had no right. Their father chose to save him over Az, and in Luc's mind, that was a mistake. Az was a much better man. But he had to admit, he was glad to see his brother alive. Their father couldn't guarantee that Gabe would be able to be revived. Just bringing Luc back was hard enough.

"I'm glad you're alive," Luc said as Gabe released him and took the seat next to him.

"As am I. I never thought Michael would do what he did. I suspected that he would try to kill you, and Az's death doesn't surprise me, but killing me wasn't anything I ever thought he would do. He's much further gone than I imagined."

"Please don't talk about him." Luc tensed again at the mention of Az.

"Michael?"

"No."

Gabe looked confused for a moment, then realization hit and he nodded. "I'm sorry. Have you seen Michael?"

"Of course not."

"I just thought that since you have him in the box, you might have gone to talk to him, to show him you were alive, at least."

"You mean to gloat? I'm not like that, despite the rumors that go around about me. I can't see him yet, but he's aware

I've been returned to the living. One day I'm sure, but not yet."

Again, Gabe nodded. Luc didn't need to explain why it was too hard for him to face Michael. Gabe already understood. If it were him, he probably would have went. Gabe liked to have the answers to all questions. He couldn't stand to have any ambiguity, but Luc was different.

He'd always been different.

"Maybe one day you can let me see him?" Gabe turned to look at Luc, but Luc kept his eyes straight ahead.

"Maybe."

"Are you the same?"

This time, Luc did turn to face Gabe, with a glare. "How could I be the same?"

"No, I mean as an angel. I'm not, my powers, I mean. Father says that with time, things may improve, but they also might not. Bringing me back was harder than he thought and he couldn't get everything back."

Luc hadn't much thought about it, but in the weeks since that night he woke up, no longer dead, he'd had a number of occasions to use his powers. Everything seemed to be working the same.

"I haven't noticed a difference."

"Oh." Gabe turned back and looked straight ahead. "I'm glad he chose you first, just so you know."

"I'm not."

Luc's words floated between them and left nothing between them but silence. Gabe sat there a few minutes longer, then got up, hugged Luc once again, and walked out. It would probably be a long time before they saw each other again. Luc had no need for Gabe now that everything was done and Gabe had no connection to Luc other than tragedy. He would come around when he hoped to see Michael. Luc already knew that would be the case.

"That's gotta hurt." Harley filled Luc's glass and he drank it down in one go.

"I'm glad he's alive."

"But you'd rather it was Az."

"Of course I would, but it's not. Dad wasted all his juice on me. He couldn't even bring Gabe back all the way and he won't even try for Az. Az was never that important to him, to any of them."

"He was to you."

Luc shook his head at her. "Don't you do that. I'm not going there, Harley."

"Deal with your grief, Lucifer. You can't just stuff it down and think it's going to go away."

"I can and I will." Luc got up from the barstool. "We aren't talking about this again."

Luc couldn't do anything *but* push his feelings down. Dealing with them, with the fact that Az was gone for good, would break him. He'd lost so much already. It was all he had in him just to deal with the fact that Anna left. Which was another thing he couldn't think about anymore. If he did, he might have to acknowledge that he cared about her, probably a bit more than any of the other girls. Or maybe quite a bit more.

But she was gone.

And so was Az.

13

"Harley, it's been weeks, and my dick is done dressing in black. Pick a girl already."

Luc paced the apartment itching to see the next pick in the mirror. This would be the first time they would pick one without Az and he was pretty sure that was the thing holding Harley up. He understood though. It pained him to go on with the game, without his brother there, cheering him on.

"Soon. Before we do that, you have some things you need to address."

"Such as?"

"That cop keeps coming by."

"Sarah Ward?"

"Yes. She just hangs around, looking for him, like some sad puppy who's owners moved away and left her behind. Someone should say something to her."

"I talked to her a few weeks ago. I told her he took off, like he wanted me to, but she didn't want to believe it. What do you expect me to do about it?"

"I don't know. Take her memories away? Tell her to get

lost? Anything that gets her out of our club so I don't have to keep looking at her. It makes me feel things and you know how I feel about that." Harley balled her fists into tight clumps.

"*Our* club, huh?"

"Is that seriously the thing you picked out of all that to focus on?"

"Oh Harley," Luc walked over to her and pulled her into a hug. She struggled against him, even punching him in the gut twice, hard, then settled in, resting her head on his chest. "It's okay to feel things."

"I don't wanna," she said with her face muffled in his shirt. She kicked him in the shin and he let her go.

"You also need to deal with Cupid. Oz came by today and he's sick of that asshole in his space. He wants you to make up your mind and decide what you want to happen to him."

Luc hadn't thought about Cupid since everything happened. To be honest, he hadn't wanted to. Luc was angry with the little shit for his part in what happened. The worst of it couldn't be pinned on him, but he still made the decision to be on Michael's side. He could say he had no choice all he wants, but if he'd come to Luc with the truth right away, and told him he needed help, Luc would have given it to him.

But he hadn't.

Part of Luc wanted to leave him with the mages forever, let them keep him locked up, hell they could toss him in a pit for all Luc cared, but that wasn't fair to them. They'd helped when Luc needed it, and probably saved some lives in the process. He also had to see Oz about his sister. In payment for his help, Luc promised to turn Oz's sister into a demon, and spring her from Hell. He wasn't looking forward to it, but he always kept his word.

"I vote that we lock him up in Hell, maybe give him a cage right next to Michael. Wouldn't it be funny to see those two stuck together as roommates for the rest of eternity?" Harley walked over to the mirror, waved her hand in front of it, and Cupid appeared in the fog. "He's trying to pretend it's all good, but I've seen him when he thinks no one is looking. He's scared shitless."

Luc waved his hand and the mirror returned to normal.

"Leave him alone."

"You're joking, right?"

"I'm not. Cupid is a piece of shit, but this isn't his fault."

"You're gonna let him go, aren't you?" Harley took a step back and narrowed her eyes.

"I haven't decided what to do with him."

"Maybe you *think* you haven't, but I can see it in your eyes. You feel bad for the little turd."

"Hasn't there been enough suffering? Luc walked over to the bar and poured his favorite bourbon. Everything was restocked, extra stocked, and back to how it should be. Not how it was, because Luc couldn't bring himself to make everything seem like nothing ever happened, but things were cleaned up and set.

"No. Az is dead."

"I'm aware." Luc cringed. "That's not something I need reminding of."

"Cupid was part of that. He should have to pay for it."

"Michael would have done what he did regardless of whether or not Cupid played a part. Was he wrong? Of course, but what can you really expect from that weasel?"

"I don't care." Harley stomped her foot like an angry toddler. "I want him to suffer for making the decisions he made. Why don't you?"

"I guess because I'm tired."

"Take a damn nap and leave Cupid locked up."

"I don't need a nap. I'm tired of the fighting, of the anger, and definitely of the bad feelings among family."

"Cupid isn't your family. Az was." Harley stressed his brother's name and Luc swallowed hard.

"Az was, you're right, but Cupid is too. And so is Michael. It doesn't matter how awful they've been, or how much I don't want it to be true. It still is."

Harley sighed. "I liked it better when you were a dick who had orgies every night."

"Sometimes twice a night."

"Those were the days." Harley gulped down her drink and headed for the door. "Take care of your shit so I don't have to hear about it. And if you let that asswipe go free, don't tell me about it."

Luc watched her shut the door behind her and slumped into his new chair. No matter what he did, it wouldn't bring Az back. He just had to deal with it now. And he had to deal with Sarah Ward, and Cupid, and Oz.

It was time.

∼

THE SAME CHATTER struck Luc when he walked into the warehouse that the mages set up shop in, but no one stopped him this time. He walked right through and back to the cages. He could feel the mages there, but for some reason, no one was making themselves known.

"Lucifer, good to see you. How have you been? No one around here tells me anything." Cupid walked over to the bars of his cage and leaned his shoulder against them. "I was starting to think you forgot about me."

"Who could forget you, *cousin*?" Luc pulled over the rusty

chair from the corner and sat down to face Cupid. He stared at him with a blank expression, and Cupid swallowed hard, shifting from one foot to the other.

"Did something happen? Did you have trouble retrieving Melanie?"

"Melanie? No. She practically begged Uriel to take her out of that psycho's place. That poor girl is back home where she belongs."

"Home? You just let her go? I don't understand." Cupid grabbed the bars with both hands and his eyes widened.

"I had her stashed in Hell for a bit, but we don't need her anymore, so her memories have been wiped, and she was sent home. Isn't that what you wanted to see happen?"

"I... well, yes. I don't like people fooling around with love. No one should be forced into it. It's unnatural."

"Some would say that angels are unnatural."

"I suppose some would, but we were here first, so they'd be wrong."

"Would they though?"

Cupid stood up straight and backed away from the cage a few feet. "What's going on?"

"Everything is over, Q. I'm actually shocked that the mages didn't tell you."

"Over? Then we won?"

"We? Who's we, because I'm never really sure which side you're on." Luc tilted his head and put one finger up to his chin.

"The side of all that's right."

"So, your own side, then? I mean, let's be honest, Q, the only thing you've ever cared about are your own needs, right?" Luc stood and walked over to the cage and Cupid backed up a few more steps. "Are you afraid of me, Q?"

"Shouldn't I be?"

"Why?"

"You're the reason I'm locked up."

"Me?" Luc threw his head back and laughed. "Oh man, you're funny tonight. I wish Harley could see this. No wait, if Harley was here, she'd probably rip your head off. As in literally."

"Why isn't she here then? Is she all right?"

"Like you care."

"Lucifer," Cupid steeled himself, then walked right up to the bars. "Is she okay?"

"She's fine. I'm sure you're happy to hear that."

"I know you won't believe this, but I'm glad she's all right."

"Are you?"

"Yes."

"Az is dead." Luc's voice had no emotion. He had to keep it that way. If he let even a second of feeling in, he would lose it.

Cupid went pale.

"Michael attacked, just like we expected, right after we took his little slave. Oh and you were right, she wasn't really in love with him."

"But you killed him?"

"He's my brother, Q. Why would I kill him? Michael is the psychopath, not me. I locked him in the Hell Box. Only not until after he killed Az and Gabe... oh and me, but dear old dad brought me back."

Cupid dropped himself into a chair. "Gabe is dead?"

"Well, he was." Luc said, tensing his shoulders. "But Dad was able to bring him back, too. Not Az though. He's gone for good. Harley thinks you should pay for your part in it, but I told her you were family, so we shouldn't just end you."

"Thanks for that." Cupid swallowed hard, making an audible sound. "He killed you?"

"He did. He jammed the forever blade right through my heart just before he was sucked into the box. I don't remember it all that well, but Uriel was there thankfully, or things would have turned out much different."

"But how—"

"How am I sitting here with you right now?"

Cupid nodded.

"Well apparently there was a little more to that blade than Dad always said. The short version, he was able to bring me back, good as new, and Gabe, not quite so good as new. Az was just shit out of luck though. Only so much juice in the old man."

"Luc, I'm so sorry. I know he was your favorite. I never meant for any of this to happen. I had no idea what a lunatic he was, or I would have come to you from the start."

"If you had, maybe things would have been different." Luc shrugged. "Maybe not."

"What are you going to do with me." Cupid's shoulders slumped forward and he looked ready to accept his fate. It was almost too easy. Luc kind of wanted him to protest, to stand up for himself, but he knew he was wrong.

"What do you think I should do to you?"

Cupid got up and walked back over to the bars. "I don't deserve to be free. I barely deserve to be alive. Maybe you should listen to Harley."

"She wants me to cage you in Hell, right next to Michael, for the rest of eternity."

"I'm surprised she didn't suggest just killing me."

"She did, but she knows I'm not willing to do that. If Michael gets to live, you certainly aren't dying for this." Luc stood and walked over to Cupid. "Look, I know you didn't mean for any of this to happen, but you fucked up big time. This isn't just a family squabble, Cupid. Az is dead. Gabe is ruined."

"And you, Lucifer, you've lost a lot too."

"That's irrelevant."

"It's not. I know I owe you for my part, and I'll accept whatever punishment you choose for me. I won't argue, or fight you. I deserve it. I would ask one thing though."

"What's that?"

"Let me find your soul mate for you. Please, just let me help, so you can find a little happiness. No one deserves it more than you."

"No." Luc tensed and ground his teeth together. The last thing he wanted, before, and definitely now, was Cupid's help finding love. He would find his soul mate without that little shit, or he would be alone forever.

"Okay. I won't push it, but if you change your mind, just say so. I'm not looking to be the hero, or anything this time. I just want to see you happy."

Luc didn't care, even if he did sound genuine.

"I'm letting you go." Luc texted Oz and asked him for the key. Seconds later, a small mage pushed past Luc, stuck a shiny key into the lock, and turned it. The lock popped and the door creaked open. She turned and left without another word.

"You're what?" Cupid's eyes bugged out of his head and he stepped back, further into the cage. "You can't."

"Of course I can."

"But—"

"Remember that part about how you won't protest or argue?"

"I know, but, that was when I thought you were going to

lock me away, send me to hell for some torture, or something awful. You can't just let me go?"

It wasn't like Cupid to care more about what was right, than his own selfish needs. Maybe the creep learned something after all.

"There's been enough awfulness in the world. I can't take anymore. Just go." Luc stepped aside and waited for Cupid to walk out of the cage. Reluctantly, he did. Before getting far, he grabbed Luc and pulled him in for a very unwanted hug.

"I won't forget your kindness, Lucifer." And with that, he was gone.

It was a weight off Luc's shoulders. Harley was going to be pissed, but she would have to get over it. Luc needed to do this.

"What about me?" Aivah called from her cell, her small voice just barely carrying.

"That's not up to me." Luc walked over and stood in front of the tiny woman. "Your fate is up to Oz, but I'll gladly tell him that in my opinion, he should go easy on you."

She stared at him, only a trace of anger still remained.

"I never meant for things to go down the way they did. I hope you can one day believe that."

She just blinked at him, so he walked away. He couldn't worry about Aivah. He would do as he said, and tell Oz not to be too harsh, but in the end, that was out of his hands. His business with Oz had nothing to do with mage insubordination.

If Oz was ready to do business, he would have come out. When he was ready, he knew where to find Luc. Until then, Luc had enough on his plate. He walked out the way he'd come in, ignoring the chatter as he passed.

∽

"I still can't believe you just let him go." Harley poured Luc a bourbon and shoved the glass at him.

"I still can't believe you haven't picked the next girl yet." Luc drank half the glass and pushed it at her to top it off. "You're the one always complaining that we need to finish and that I can't take time off. I think it's time, Harley."

"I know. I just wanted to make sure I picked the right one this time. You don't need to deal with anyone else's problems this month."

"Just pick who you would have picked if none of this happened. I can handle it. I won't break."

"Yeah, yeah, I know. You're the King of Hell and all that jazz. You're big and strong, and tough."

"No. I'm just doing the best I can, same as you. I miss Az, too. I know this is hard."

"Yeah, whatever." Harley flipped the bar towel over her shoulder and started stacking glasses.

She'd been pissy since he went to see Cupid. Hell, she'd been pissy for weeks, but Luc understood. She had to grieve in her own way. They really were all just doing the best they could.

"Mr. Morningstar?"

Luc spun around to find Sarah Ward standing behind him. Her hair was down, sitting in long tangles around her shoulders, and she was dressed in jeans and a t-shirt. She looked tired and sad.

"Detective Ward, how nice to see you. Is something wrong?"

"Have you seen your brother?" Desperation didn't look good on her, but Luc felt bad for the woman. He wanted so badly to tell her the truth, that Az was dead and he was never coming back. But he had to respect his brother's last wishes.

"I haven't. I'm sorry. He can be a flake sometimes, but it's only because he really cared about you. It scared him, ya know?"

She nodded, but there was no sign of recognition.

"Az has a serious fear of commitment. Always has. I'm so sorry you got caught up in that."

"But when will he be back?"

Luc closed his eyes and let out a soft breath, then he did something he rarely did. He put his hand on the side of her face and spoke in a soft, soothing, tone. "He's not coming back. He's a jerk, and you still care about him, but it's time to move on. You can't just wait around for someone who isn't here. If he was, it would be different, but he's not." Luc dropped his hand and she blinked a few times. "You're going to be okay."

She nodded. "I'm okay." She stood in front of Luc a few more seconds, then turned, and headed out the front door.

It hurt Luc to watch her go. It was like saying goodbye to the last piece of Az. He cared about that woman. For maybe the first time ever, Az had found someone he wanted to be with for more than a few nights. He might even have loved her. But none of that mattered now. He was gone and she needed to move on.

"Did you just use your powers on her?" Harley grabbed the back of Luc's shirt and pulled him so he turned to look at her.

"Yeah. She's not part of the game, so I didn't break any rules."

"Even if you had, I'd still be proud of you." It was the closest Harley came to feelings and Luc understood how much that meant.

It's what Az would have wanted, what he would have done for Luc if the situation was reversed. His brother was gone, and as hard as that was to accept, all he could do now was honor him. He would do that by finishing the game and looking out for the woman he cared about. He would do it by living his life, finding his soul mate, and not letting tragedy take everything from him once again.

Luc finished off his drink and pushed the glass away. He was ready for a new start. With two more sins to go, he would give it his best shot, or at least the best he could manage. He couldn't let Michael ruin the game that Az was so excited for. He had to get to the end, then he would ask Harley which sin Az knew he'd pick, because Luc already knew he would be right.

THANK YOU FOR READING!

Thank You for Reading!

If you enjoyed this, or any of my books, please take a moment to leave a review. They are so helpful in getting the word out there and helping others decide if a book might be worth their time. If you have any suggestions, ideas, problems, or just want to say hi, please feel free to look me up on Facebook, Twitter, or Instagram.

Facebook.com/AuthorLJBaker
    Twitter: @AuthorLJBaker
    Instagram: AuthorLJBaker

I'd love to hear your thoughts on what you'd like to see in future books, so please feel free to send me off a message, email, tweet, or dm me on Instagram and let me know what you think.

Thank you for taking your precious time to read my books. I appreciate it with all my heart.

BOOKS BY LJ BAKER

Ages 13+

Save Me (Life After the Outbreak, book 1)
Find Me (Life After the Outbreak, book 2)
Hold Me (Life After the Outbreak, book 3)

Stand Alone Books

Time Curse
The Clinic

18+ Only!

Undeniable (Bound Together, book 1)
Inevitable (Bound Together, book 2)
Unavailable (Bound Together, book 3)
Incapable (Bound Together, book 4)
Intolerable (Bound Together, book 5)
Unbearable (Bound Together, book 6)

Taking Chances (Learning to love, book 1)

Wrath (Seven Deadly Sins, book 1)
Gluttony (Seven Deadly Sins, book 2)
Greed (Seven Deadly Sins, book 3)
Sloth (Seven Deadly Sins, book 4)

Lust (Seven Deadly Sins, book 5)

Pride (Seven Deadly Sins, book 6)

Envy (Seven Deadly Sins, book 7)

ACKNOWLEDGMENTS

Out of all the books in this series, this was the one I was both looking forward to the most, and dreading. Losing someone you care about is hard. It wrecks your whole world. It takes everything away from you. Finding a way to move forward after that seems impossible. There are a few people that I have to acknowledge that have made it possible for me to start to find that place in my own world.

As always, I need to thank my bratty kid, Jennylee, who lets me talk about my crazy characters and drone on about my ideas, even when she would rather not listen. She manages to read my books and help me whip them into shape so that I can share them with all of you. If it wasn't for her, I wouldn't be writing this right now.

I also need to thank my other brats and husband for being in my life and providing an endless source of amusement, irritation, and general emotional background to draw upon when I need to write about feelings. You idiots have made sure I can relate to just about any feeling the devil himself might need to experience. I love you.

Lastly, I need to throw in a thank you to my therapist, who never ceases to see the world in a much better light than reality casts upon it. Without him, I probably wouldn't have anyone to argue with that didn't hold it against me. He might get paid to talk to me, but he's worth every penny.

ABOUT THE AUTHOR

L J lives on the Jersey Shore with her husband, bratty kid and two crazy cats. Though writing has always been her first passion, she got a degree in psychological counseling and worked in the mental health field for a while, which she finds very helpful in dealing with her crazy family. She is a lover of all different types of music and books, switching between genres so wildly it sometimes makes people wonder if she has multiple personalities. She is most likely to be found writing romance stories of all kinds (contemporary, erotic, new adult, young adult, fantasy, paranormal, etc.). When she's not writing, she prefers to spend her time reading, taking photos, watching way too much television, or spending time with her family.

She would love to hear what you think of her work or answer any questions you might have. Please feel free to visit her and say hi.

Facebook.com/AuthorLJBaker
  Twitter: @AuthorLJBaker
  Instagram: AuthorLJBaker
  www.lj-baker.com.